Night Journey

H. Scott Butler

High Tide Publications
Deltaville, Virginia

High Tide Publications, Inc.
1000 Bland Point Road
Deltaville, Virginia 23043
www.HighTidePublications.com

Publisher's Note: This is a work of fiction. Names, characters, places, and incidents are a product of the author's imagination. Locales and public names are sometimes used for atmospheric purposes. Any resemblance to actual people, living or dead, or to businesses, companies, events, institutions, or locales is completely coincidental.

Edited by: Narielle Living

Technical Advisor: Detective Salvatore Franco, Suffolk County, NY (RIP)

Cover Photograph: Eldercroft, N.C.

Book Design: FireBelliedFrog.com

Night Journey/H Scott Butler 2nd ed.

Printed in the United States of America

For Susan

Paragraph: Garamond 11pt, 11.871 leading

Chapter Heading: Latin Modern Dunhill roman 24 pt , 28.8 leading

Margins: 1" top, 1" inside, .75 outside, .75 bottom. No gutter

Page placement: Chapter Heading has 2.5 lead from top margin

First paragraph: font to match heading (Latin Modern Dunhill roman at 11 pt with a drop cap of 3/1.

Heading:

Left Header: Page number left justified/author name 8 point to match chapter heading Latin Modern Dunhill Roman

Right Header: Page number justified right/ book title 8 point to match chapter heading Latin Modern Dunhill Roman

Follow blank page as necessary/ chapter always on right (odd number page) not heading on chapter or blank pages.

Chapter 1

*S*he should *see* him now, he thinks, as he examines his chiseled upper body, shiny with sweat, in the closet-door mirror. She always mocked him for being puny, and he was puny. When he got his first barbell set two years ago, he could barely lift 130 pounds. Now he does lifts of 200 pounds and overhead presses of 110. And he might even be further along if he trained at a well-equipped gym. But he's chosen to keep his muscularity a secret. Maybe he's being overly cautious, but it seems wise not to call attention to himself in any way, and since he has the sort of modest frame that turns ordinary clothing into a disguise, why not use this to his advantage? Besides, he's already achieved his strength goal.

He lies down on the exercise mat, raises his knees, and comes up slowly, focusing the work in his abs and counting to himself at the top of each sit-up. After a few minutes a faint whiff of his own sweat reminds him of the smell of the nursing home, that strong urinal tang in the stifling air. He remembers how it seemed to fume off the pale yellow, piss-colored walls. When he complained about it once to his mother, she called him an ungrateful little shit—little shit being the constant in her rebukes. But it was hard to feel gratitude for having to sit so many hours in the nursing-home lobby among the stinking, toothless old wrecks in their wheelchairs. Most of them were zombies, empty-eyed and open-mouthed, but there was always at least one with just enough brain left to harass him with some crazy request repeated over and over. He would make faces at them, not that it ever did any good, and when he could get away with it, he'd escape by roaming the building. This wasn't much of an improvement over sitting in the lobby; the smell was even worse beyond the double doors that led to the main hallway. But occasionally he'd come across something of interest, like the time he opened the door to a room and saw Elroy the janitor with an old woman.

Elroy was a skinny little man with rabbit teeth and no chin. He had a high-pitched *giggle, and his country accent sounded like grunts and gargles. Momma called him a white trash moron. But the Elroy he saw that day was transformed. He'd pulled the old woman around to the side of her bed and was vigorously thrusting his shirt-tail-covered buttocks between her bare legs. She, meanwhile, her face hidden, was making low moaning noises like someone trapped in a nightmare. At the time he was too young to fully comprehend Elroy's purpose, but there was no mistaking his power and decisiveness.*

He remembers another door-opening episode that happened a few years later, when he could stay by himself after school. He was eager to tell his mother about his perfect score on a math test, but she called to say she had a meeting with Mr. Dent and hung up before he could give her his news. He ordered pizza and paid for it with the coffee-canister money, as he was allowed to do in the circumstances, finished his homework, watched some TV, and finally got in bed around midnight. He was still awake, however, when he heard her in the hall. She hated any interruption to her routines, so he gave her time to take a bath and get ready for bed. Then he went down to her room. He could hear her radio playing, but not wanting to wake her if she'd drifted off, he opened the door quietly. She wasn't asleep, or in bed. She was sitting at her dressing table brushing her hair, and she was naked except for a pair of pink panties. She must have seen him in the mirror because she spun around with a scowl on her face. At the sight of her breasts, his thing jerked in his pajamas, but it was the only part of him capable of movement. He watched her leap up and march toward him, her breasts jiggling. Her nipples were pink in pink circles. She was gripping the hairbrush, and when she reached him, she hit him hard with it in the crotch. As he doubled over, screaming and grabbing himself, she said, "That will teach you to knock, you filthy-minded little shit."

He realizes he's lost count of the sit-ups. He may have reached a hundred, but it's important to maintain a sense of discipline. That's how he's come so far so fast. He begins over, and when he's counted off a hundred, he rolls out the barbell and slides on extra discs for the dead lifts. Staring down at the bar, he feels a slight sense of disappointment. He's put considerable effort into being able to do what he does—lift a woman weighing 120 or 130 who was still seizing from the shock of the stun gun, elbow open the popped trunk, toss her in, cuff and gag her, all in a few seconds time. But this achievement is only the means to an end, and the end, so far, hasn't quite lived up to his expectations. The women he selected had seemed so sure of themselves, so smugly in control of their lives. It's the main reason he picked them. His plan was to strip away their confidence bit by bit. He imagined them offering him money, promising they wouldn't say anything, telling him they knew he wasn't really like this, reminding him of the executioner's needle, treating him like the stupid little man they thought he was. He'd pretend to be affected by their words; he'd express remorse for what he was doing to them, though continuing to do it of course. And so it would take them some time to realize his complete mastery of them. But he wasn't allowed this pleasure. Once he had them in his power, they put up no resistance at all, unless you counted begging; their self-assurance vanished like a mirage. Not that he considers his time with them wasted. Far from it. The second stage, as he thinks of it, has its own pleasures, the main one being rooted in necessity: to keep them from turning into zombies, you have to dole out some hope and relief, which adds a certain psychological interest. But even so, he won't be satisfied until he's fulfilled his first-stage fantasy.

Ironically, the closest he's come, from the standpoint of encountering resistance, was in his initial, botched attempt at a kidnapping. Everything went wrong. As soon as the bitch saw his knife, she started screaming and pulling away, and he was forced to use it on her—only to discover that he was too weak to drag her out of sight. He had to jump in his car and drive off with the body in plain view. For months afterward he lived in fear of the police knocking on his door. Yet in retrospect that single deep slash was more thrilling than anything he's done since. Her trophy is the one that still excites him the most.

He does ten dead lifts. Then he carries his dumbbells over to the mirror and begins a set of curls, watching his biceps bulge, relax, bulge. She's out there somewhere, he thinks. The woman who'll cling to her sense of superiority until he's shown her it doesn't exist. This time he'll get it right.

Chapter 2

The call came in around five on a Monday morning, just as Cynthia was finishing up a report on a man who'd gone over a balcony railing in a shoving match, so drunk he'd only sprained his ankle— the usual sort of case she worked in her part of Northern Virginia.

"Westbrook, county sheriff's," she said.

"Oh, yeah," the caller said. "This is Epps, North Hill police. Your partner there?"

"If you mean Ed, he retired."

"Lemme speak to the new one, then."

"You have something to say, Officer Epps, say it to me."

"Well, we got a situation here looks like another kidnapping."

"How so?"

"Unlocked car, groceries on the back seat, owner's purse on the ground."

"Who's the owner?"

"White female, thirty-two."

"You try calling her?"

"Yeah. No landline, and her cell's in the purse."

"Did you check the county hospital?"

"Only female admitted last night was from a nursing home."

"Okay. You touch anything besides her purse?"

"No, nothing," he said.

"Good." She'd have to get his prints anyway, and those of any other cops at the scene. "Seal it off, say twenty feet out from the car. And stay clear of anything that might be evidence—a cigarette butt, candy wrapper, whatever. Address?"

"Greenwood Shopping Center, off of—"

"I know where it is. Twenty minutes."

Jeff, who'd already slipped on his sport coat, said, "Another abduction?"

"Could be." Cynthia called the lab tech on standby, waking him, and told him to meet them there. Larry, the tech, was an irascible type; he'd be pissed if this turned out to be a false alarm. But in case it wasn't, she wanted as fast a start as possible.

As she drove them through the early morning dark, Jeff said, "What about Roger?"

"Let's see what we've got before we talk to Roger." The first abduction had occurred on January 9 in Parkerville, in a fitness center parking lot just a couple of miles from headquarters. She and Ed caught the case and worked it, without success, and when there was a second disappearance in North Hill on May 21, the sheriff requested FBI assistance.

The feds came in force, a bunch of self-important men and one woman with more attitude than the men. They set up a command post in the sheriff's office and took over the tip line, and within three weeks brought in a person of interest. But they didn't have anything solid on him, and when he didn't break under interrogation as they'd expected, they packed up and dumped the case back in the department's lap. A month later Ed suffered a mild heart attack and decided to retire. Maybe he really quit for the sake of his health, but he also resented the whole FBI episode. And since he wasn't happy about working with a woman, either—she'd come from Property Crimes just before the first disappearance—he probably wanted to get away from her too. His absence created an awkward situation. The cases were hers, but she was a homicide rookie. Instead of removing her outright, Major Sampson put Roger in charge of tips, by then the only active aspect of the investigations. On her own time she'd stayed with the abductions, looking for connections between the victims and keeping tabs on the person of interest. She'd also persuaded Roger to let her and her new partner follow up on the most promising tips, although none of them had led anywhere.

"If it is another one," Jeff said, "then what?"

"We took the call. We'll just keep moving until somebody says stop."

"Juking and jiving."

"Right."

In the Escort's dark interior Jeff began to hum, his hand tapping out the rhythm on his thigh. On the strength of his record he'd jumped straight from uniform to Crimes Against Persons. He was the youngest investigator in the division and the only African American, a double coup. But she knew he missed the daily excitement of patrol, the drug busts and chase-downs, the crazies brandishing knives and Chihuahuas. So at the moment, and despite having been up all night, he was a happy man.

She turned into the shopping center lot and drove past a lone cart, its red handle-grip flashing in the headlights. The abandoned car was sitting in the middle of the shadowy pavement with two black-and-whites near it and unsecured crime tape around it. Fortunately, there was no breeze. She parked outside the tape and they walked over to the cops, who'd gotten out of their cars. The fat, bald one with the Gordon Liddy mustache was Epps. She knew him from the previous North Hill disappearance. He'd taken his cue from Ed in how he treated her but added his own twist. Whereas Ed always responded to her, though usually with a surprised look as if he'd forgotten she was capable of speech, Epps just ignored her.

"Officer Epps," she said.

Looking past her, he nodded.

"This is Investigator White," she said, introducing Jeff.

"White," Epps said to him, with a tad too much emphasis on the name.

"Eeps," Jeff said.

"It's Epps," said Epps.

"Oops," said Jeff.

The other cop, a good-looking young guy, gave them a conspiratorial smile.

She took a deep breath of the chilly air. Ed had treated her like crap, but he'd also been a good detective, and she'd learned some things by watching him. One was to take your time. She scanned the parking lot lamps for surveillance cameras and didn't see any. She looked at the storefronts aligned under a gray mansard roof. The grocery was the anchor building, with a pizza joint, movie rental, and dry cleaner on one side, and a state liquor store and a dollar store on the other. Lights on the mansard made the signage visible. The windows of the grocery and the dollar store revealed un-peopled interiors in a melancholy dimness.

In the dark restaurant window, lighted neon lettering spelled out PIZZA, the red glow bleeding into the gloom.

She turned her attention to the car, a green Volkswagen Beetle. A black leather bag, unzipped, sat beside it on the ground.

"This where you found the purse?" she said.

"It was under the car," Epps said. "Williams saw a piece of the strap."

Using her flashlight, she scanned the pavement and the side of the car for signs of blood or anything else unusual. She peered through the raised windows. There was a folded camel coat on the back seat and two beige plastic bags on the floor. Celery leaves sprouted from the nearer one. She pulled out her digital camera and took some shots through the glass. Then she put on the latex gloves she'd stuffed in her jacket pocket, opened the driver's door, and leaned in. Nothing caught her eye except the tidiness. And the absence of keys. The victim wouldn't have put them back in her purse. She searched the floor and the space under the front seat. Nothing there, not even a candy wrapper. She opened the back door and felt in the pockets of the coat. Empty.

"See any keys?" she said to the cops.

"Nope," Epps said, "but I did observe a suspicious cigarette butt over there." With a smirk he pointed to a spot near the tape.

She gave Jeff a let-it-go look and went down on one knee and shone her light under the car. There they were, nestled against the inside of the opposite front tire. The yellow smiley face key chain was smiling sideways at her.

"Found 'em," she said. She aimed the camera at them and snapped.

Jeff kneeled beside her and looked, then went around to retrieve the keys. When he came back, he said, "So she puts the groceries in the back and takes off her coat—"

"She could have left it in the car. Last night wasn't very cold."

"Okay. Then she's grabbed, probably, since she drops her stuff."

"Which the perp or perps kick under the car. That's a difference from the other two crime scenes. We found a purse out in the open at one and a shoe at the other."

"Smoother operation this time. More confidence."

Cynthia nodded. She kneeled again and, holding her light over the purse, rummaged through its meager contents. The only items of interest were a spiral memo pad, a red leather wallet, and the cell. She looked in the pad. It was blank. She opened the wallet. The cash sleeve held four twenties and three ones, and two credit cards were in the cardholder.

Robbery wouldn't seem to figure even as a secondary motive. There was also some sort of an ID. She slipped it out. It was a faculty ID for Mary Weaver College. The picture showed a pretty, slender-faced young woman with large brown eyes, shoulder-length brown hair, and the faintest of smiles. The same physical type as the other victims. The name beside the picture was Alicia Bradford.

Handing Jeff the card, she said to Epps, "Where's the driver's license?"

"Oh." He pulled it out of his jacket pocket and gave it to her. The face in the photo had the same expression. The date of birth made Alicia Bradford thirty-two, as Epps had said—he could do simple math, unless Williams had done it for him. The other victims were also in their thirties.

She wrote the address in her notebook, took out the cell and clicked through the saved numbers. There were four of them, all identified by first names only. No In Case of Emergency. She wrote down the names and numbers.

"Be good to know her department at Mary Weaver," she said.

"I'll take a crack at it," Williams said, and climbed in his black-and-white.

She stuck her head into the back of the car again and scrabbled through the grocery bags until she found a receipt. The time stamp said 10/10/10 7:41 p.m. Like the other two women, Alicia had vanished in darkness.

She wrote the time down. A raucous noise drew her gaze to the dark trees behind the shopping center. Dozens of crows were flying out of them, their shifting shapes dissolving into the gray sky. "Are there woods back there?" she said.

"Just a neighborhood buffer," Epps said.

Williams reemerged and handed her a slip of paper. "English department," he said. "Allen Hall. I wrote down the office number and the phone number too."

She thanked him and punched the number on her cell. After four rings Alicia's voice, soft and formal, offered the standard apology and asked the caller to leave a message. She hung up.

Jeff, meanwhile, had begun taking pictures of the Volks. While he was doing this, a car turned into the lot and nearly rammed the derelict shopping cart. It pulled up beside the Escort, and Larry got out carrying his forensics bag. A goodly portion of his auburn comb-over was floating cloud-like to one side of his head.

"Looks like we've got a crime scene," she said to him.

"I should fucking hope we've got a crime scene," he said.

"Collect everything on the ground inside the tape, but pay special attention to this area here by the car, where it looks like she was taken. And dust the door for prints."

"Tell me something I didn't already think of," Larry said.

"You forgot to comb your hair," Jeff said.

"Oh, shit." Larry pawed at his head.

"No. Yeah. That's better," Jeff said, though the unruly strands had resumed their hovering as soon as Larry removed his hand.

"Looks good," Williams deadpanned.

"Jeff, if you'll give Larry a hand," she said, "I'll pay a visit to the college."

"With pleasure," Jeff said. "Larry's a fun guy."

"Fuck you," Larry said.

"We should also do something about securing this tape," she said.

"I could ask for some cones to weigh it down," Williams said.

"Good idea." She glanced up at the trees over the mansard. Their green and yellow foliage shone faintly now, as if shrouded in mist. "Long shot," she said, "but you might check those woods."

"Waste of time," Epps said.

But when Williams started off on foot, Epps, muttering to himself, hitched his gear belt and followed. "See about getting their prints," she said to Jeff.

Driving out of the lot she saw a bus pull into the stop on Second Street and a handful of women, Hispanic by the look of them, get off. Blue maid's dresses showed beneath their coats. They'd be picked up here and driven to the gated neighborhood north of the city, where lawyers and doctors and the higher paid college personnel lived. Those still on the bus would be working people too, on their way to low-wage jobs at places like the college and the nursing home. Most of them would have come from a little town called Calvary that was an anomaly in horse country, lacking as it did boutiques and antique shops and signs with the words horse, fox, or hound in them. It had always been a sort of down-at-the-heels working-class town, and now it was evolving into a Hispanic working-class town, which might be the saving of it. Years ago she'd made the trip from Calvary to North Hill to attend classes at Mary Weaver, arriving early in the morning and taking the last bus back.

Chapter 3

Cynthia parked on the curb in front of the cream-colored administration building and walked around it past the colonnaded library to Allen Hall, the humanities building, a red brick structure with a fanlight over the door. On a nearby bench a young man sat with his eyes closed and his hands in the pockets of his hoodie. Sleeping one off? Campus security would have rousted him. Waiting for a girl, maybe, whom he might be in danger of missing. When she was a student here, Mary Weaver was still a women's college. She went up the steps and entered the foyer. At the center of the black-veined marble floor was a broad, white marble staircase that gave way, she knew, to second and third flights of ordinary wooden stairs with rubber runners. The English Department occupied the top floor.

As she ascended the echoing stairwells, she remembered carrying a late paper to slip under Dr. Ruth Ayers's door. It was as if she were recalling someone else's life. She opened the door upon a ghostly image of herself—a lone, rangy woman in slacks and a leather jacket—staring from the dark glass of the English office. She went down the creaking hall in search of office number 319 and found it near the end. A framed card on the door showed Alicia Bradford's name, office hours, and work and cell phone numbers. Not expecting an answer, she knocked. She gave it a moment and went back to the stairway door and waited for someone to show up. Her late paper, she remembered, had been on Wallace Stevens's "The Idea of Order at Key West." It was one of the last papers she'd written before shifting her attention to the idea of order in Harris County.

After a while she heard the relaxed murmur of voices on the stairs, and two women came through the door. One of them was Dr. Ayers. She'd gone gray and put on weight in the intervening years, but her green-eyed, latte-colored face wasn't much altered except for a deep vertical crease between her eyebrows.

Cynthia unclipped her badge from her belt and identified herself. "I'm looking for Alicia Bradford," she said. "Have either of you seen or heard from her this morning?"

Both women shook their heads, and Dr. Ayers said, "Is something wrong?"

"She may be missing. Her car was found in a parking lot this morning."

The other woman, a middle-aged white woman, put her hand to her mouth, but Dr. Ayers merely looked distracted. Cynthia remembered that expression from her lectures; she'd stand for a moment with lips parted and eyes downcast as she collected her thoughts.

"Maybe it wouldn't start and she had to leave it," Dr. Ayers said.

"We don't think so."

"I'll just go to her office and—"

"I've already done that. Does she have a class this morning?"

"I believe so, but I'll check," said the other woman. She unlocked the door to the office and switched on the light. They followed her to the secretary's desk, presumably hers. She opened a side drawer and pulled out a sheet. "Yes, she has an eight o'clock."

Cynthia glanced at her watch: 7:38. "If she's coming, she should be here soon."

"Yes," the woman said.

"What about the hospital?" Dr. Ayers said. "Maybe she had an accident and—"

"We checked."

"I'm sorry. It's just that…"

"I know," Cynthia said.

Their eyes met, and Dr. Ayers gave her a funny look.

"There were a few names in her cell phone, no last names," Cynthia said. She took out her notebook. "Laura. Does that mean anything to either of you?"

"It could be me," the secretary said.

Cynthia read her the number.

"Yes, that's my number here."

"And you're the department secretary—is that why she'd have it?"

"I guess so."

"How about Mike?"

They shook their heads.

"Ruth?" she said, looking at Dr. Ayers. She read the number aloud.

"My office phone," Dr. Ayers said.

"Are the two of you friends?"

"No, not really. I'm the current department chair. I suppose that's why…"

"Sam and Susan, together?"

They shook their heads again.

"The last one is Walt."

Dr. Ayers's light cheeks colored. "Well, there's a Walter in the department. Walter Lewis."

Cynthia read them the number. Laura, consulting another sheet, said, "It's his home number."

"What's their relationship?"

The two women exchanged glances.

"They're friends, I believe," Dr. Ayers said.

"Just friends?"

"As far as I know."

"Anything to add to that?" Cynthia said to Laura.

"I've seen them talking, that's all."

"When does Walter Lewis come in?"

Laura looked at the class schedule again. "He has his poetry writing class at three. He might be in sooner."

"He's a poet?" Cynthia said.

"Yes," Dr. Ayers said. "Surely, you don't think that he…"

"I don't think anything yet. Let's give Alicia a few more minutes."

"Yes. Of course."

Laura gestured at the two chairs against the wall. "We could sit down," she said.

She rolled her own chair around the desk, and they sat together and waited.

"When was the last time you saw her?" Cynthia asked.

"Friday afternoon," Dr. Ayers said. "Passing in the hall. We said hello."

"She came in here around four to pick up her mail," Laura said. "I asked if she had any plans for the weekend, and she smiled and said grading papers."

"She didn't seem upset or worried about anything?"

"No. Just the opposite. She was serene almost."

"How about in recent weeks? A student give her a hard time or anything like that?"

"No, not to my knowledge," Dr. Ayers said. She looked at Laura, who shook her head.

"What's she like?" Cynthia said.

Dr. Ayers considered this.

"Quiet. Rather private. Very earnest about her work. She specializes in children's literature."

"How long has she been here?"

"She came last year."

"Boyfriend?"

"Not that I'm aware of."

"Is Walter Lewis married?"

"He is married, yes," Dr. Ayers said in a neutral voice.

Cynthia checked her watch. Alicia Bradford should be here by now. But if she were, how could she explain her abandoned car and the dropped purse and keys? What story could she tell?

"Excuse me," Dr. Ayers said, "but have we met before?"

"I was a student of yours fourteen years ago," Cynthia said. "Your modern poetry class."

"Oh, my."

"I enjoyed it very much."

"Good. Thank you."

"And you didn't dock me for a late paper I slipped under your door one evening."

Dr. Ayers's fleeting smile left in its wake a deeper furrow above her nose. With a little shake of her head she said, "Such a strange morning. I can't wrap my mind around it."

Cynthia looked at her watch again. "It's ten after," she said.

"I should dismiss her class," Laura said. "But what do I tell them?"

"Don't tell them anything yet." She gave each of them her card. "If Alicia shows up or contacts you, have her call me."

"Please find her," Dr. Ayers said.

"I'll do my best."

Chapter 4

Alicia's classroom was on the second floor. Cynthia, walking down with Laura, asked where Lewis's office was.

"He's two doors down from Alicia," Laura said.

"What's your impression of him?"

"I don't know. He's nice, I guess."

"Something about him bother you?"

"No, it's just… this is his first term here, so I haven't seen that much of him."

"Where'd he come from?"

"Portland University, in Oregon. He was writer in residence there."

"When did he move here?"

"In the summer. Late June."

They reached the exit. "Was he here earlier for an interview or anything?" Cynthia said.

Laura looked at her as if she'd realized the implication. "No. Ruth—Dr. Ayers—interviewed him at a conference. In Houston, I believe."

"Thanks," Cynthia said.

Laura suddenly burst into tears. She pulled a tissue from her sweater pocket and dabbed at her eyes.

Cynthia waited for her to calm down.

"I'm all right," Laura said after a moment. "Are my eyes red?"

"Not much."

"Well. It could be an allergy, couldn't it?"

Laura went through the door, and Cynthia continued down the stairs. When she got to the car, she called Jeff.

"Nothing in the woods," he told her. "Eeps stepped in a hole and twisted his ankle."

"Too bad."

"Yeah, it's a real shame. Williams got the next shift to bring some traffic cones to put on the tape. Larry's packing up. He still looks like a mad scientist."

She laughed. "I'm going to call Roger, and then I'll come get you."

"Okay. Grocery store's open. Thought I'd scout it out."

"Maybe you can get the IDs copied there before Larry takes everything away."

"Good idea."

She phoned Roger and made her report.

"Jesus," he said. "I've fucking had it with these fucking disappearances."

Roger, who was bucking for captain, considered his association with the abductions a liability. Before he stopped feeling sorry for himself and focused on her, she said, "We're going to the woman's apartment, and if we don't find her there, we'll track down the guy the feds couldn't nail."

"Uh, okay. I'll talk to Sampson."

Ignoring this, she asked for a crew to canvass the shopping center.

"I'll organize it," he said gloomily.

"Thanks. Larry will have two ID photos you can use for fliers."

Alicia's car was still in the lot, awaiting the flatbed to take it to headquarters. Despite the tape, the added cones, and a black-and-white on the perimeter, the Volkswagen seemed less forlorn in the daylight. Morning sun glinted off its bubbly cartoon shape. The little engine that could. But its presence signified that a terrible thing had happened, could still be happening. If they ever learned the details, they'd reduce them to the clinical terms of a police report; and if they ever caught the killer, the prosecutor would take their language and pump it full of false emotion. Like cops, prosecutors of homicides could only give so much of themselves to the pain of others. They protected themselves from the horror they wanted to make a jury feel, and so the jurors who did feel it got there by other means, the crime-scene photos or the testimony.

Cynthia parked near the grocery store entrance and went inside. Jeff was at the customer service desk chatting with a pug-nosed young woman who bore a resemblance to the happy pig logo on her shirt. She was staring at him in the attentive, wide-eyed way that females of whatever age tended to do. Although he was a good half-foot shorter than Cynthia's six-foot-two-inches, he was handsome and strongly built—he'd been a star running back in high school before he damaged his knee—and he capitalized on these assets with his sense of humor and genuine liking of women, a rarity in her experience of men.

"This is Christine," he told her.

"Hiah!" Christine chirped.

"Christine's been a big help. She made blowups of the IDs, and she put together a list of who was working last night. Plus, she got us the interior surveillance tapes from yesterday."

Cynthia thanked her, and Jeff smiled and said, "See you, Christine."

Beaming at him, she said, "Bye, bye, now."

Once they were through the door, Cynthia said breathily, "Bye, bye, now."

Jeff grinned. "Nice girl."

"You think every girl is nice."

"I don't think you're so nice."

"I'm no girl."

"Then that Williams must have the hots for grannies. He sure gave you the once over."

"What were you doing looking at Williams?"

"I'm naturally observant. That's why I'm gonna make sergeant before you do."

She opened the trunk, got the GPS from her gear bag, and handed it to him. "Okay, Hawkeye, plug in Alicia Bradford's address. I'll read it to you."

"Yessum."

She filled him in on her college visit as she drove.

"So Lewis is out for the first two," he said.

"Unless we find some airline tickets."

"Besides, he's a poet. I mean, he spends his days rhyming *moon* with

June."

"Like Milton," she said.

He regarded her with suspicion. "Did Milton rhyme?"

"Not in *Paradise Lost*, anyway."

The apartment was only a few miles behind the shopping center in a smallish brick complex with green shutters. They knocked on Alicia's door and then got the manager to let them in.

"We're just looking for Alicia," she said to Jeff. "But you see anything of search warrant interest, make a mental note."

Tidiness here, too. Bare coffee table and lamp table, and in the kitchen area at the back mostly bare counters. A room to the right served as a study, with a laptop and a printer on a little desk and four wooden bookcases against the walls. Nothing in the wastebaskets. The extra bathroom off the kitchen looked unused; there was no hand towel on the rack or soap on the sink. The bedroom was similarly Spartan except for a blue quilt of multi-fabric stars folded on the end of the bed and two pictures hanging side-by-side.

The larger of the two, an oil painting, showed a farmhouse at dusk with dark trees behind it and a long meadow in the foreground. Narrowing slabs of thick gray paint, like an ice floe moving into the distance, formed the meadow. The trees were black dabs against a murky violet sky. The house, a thinly painted, pale blank shape, had the air of a ghost ship on an icy sea. The other picture was a lovingly detailed ink drawing of two light-haired girls. They were standing in front of a tree, its fallen leaves all around them, and they looked solemn but not unhappy, as though they understood they were being immortalized. She put their ages at around four and six. The younger one was dressed in a tiara and a puffy-sleeved princess dress. The older one, peering through dark-frame glasses, wore a homemade sorcerer's hat—the drawing conveyed its papery texture and amateurish stars—and a robe that looked like the bedroom quilt. The bottom of the robe piled at her hidden feet upon the leaves. Something about her eyes suggested Alicia.

"Is that her?" Jeff said, pointing to the sorceress.

"Could be."

Cynthia listened for a moment to the silence. What sounds would have filled it normally? The tap-tap of a keyboard. The muted shushing of the shower. The radio beside the bed turned low. She could imagine only such modest signs of Alicia's presence, like ripples on the surface of a lake. But the absence of those ripples felt absolute.

"Time to find out who those other cell-phone contacts are," she said.

"We could split it up," Jeff offered without enthusiasm. There was no pleasure in being the bearer of bad news.

"That's okay, I'll do it." She took out her notebook and found the phone list. "Neither area code is local," she said. "410 and 617."

"410 is Baltimore, or it includes Baltimore. I've got some relatives there."

She punched in the number. After the fifth ring, a male voice, rough and groggy, said, "Yeah?"

"Is this Mike?"

"Who's this?"

"Cynthia Westbrook, Harris County sheriff's investigator. I'm calling about Alicia Bradford."

"Alicia?" There was a clattering noise. "What happened?"

"She appears to be missing. North Hill police found her car in a parking lot this morning."

"When?"

"Around five."

"So you've already checked the places she might be."

Surprised by this observation, she said, "The ones we could think of, yes. We're at her apartment now. Could you tell me who you are?"

"Her uncle."

"I also don't know your last name. It wasn't in her cell."

"You got her cell? Christ. What about her purse?"

"I'm not at liberty to—"

"Fallon," he said.

Writing this down, she said, "Have you been in touch with her recently?"

She heard a shaky intake of breath. "A few days ago," he said. "Tuesday, I think it was."

"She mention any concerns or worries? Anything that frightened her?"

"No, but…those women who disappeared—it was in the papers here, and after the second one I got her some pepper spray. I also tried to talk her into carrying stronger protection, a Taser or a handgun. She wasn't interested, but last week she called and asked me to recommend a gun."

"Why'd she change her mind?"

"I kept asking her that. But all she'd say was she'd decided I was right."

"How'd she sound?"

"Okay. Normal. But I don't know her all that well. Until she moved there, I hadn't seen her in years, not since she was a kid. And we don't have much common—a college teacher and a cop."

"You're a cop?"

"Was. Thirty years with the Baltimore police, last sixteen in homicide."

If this was a veiled offer of help, she hoped it would stay that way. "Did she buy a gun?"

"I don't know. I told her when she did to call me and I'd come show her how to use it. But she never called."

"What kind of gun did you recommend?"

In a heavy voice, he said, ".38 Special. Short-nosed."

"One more question, Mr. Fallon. Do you know who Sam and Susan are?"

"Yeah, Sam and Susan Bradford. Her uncle and aunt on her father's side. Sam's her father's brother. When she was ten, her family was killed in a car accident, and she went to live with them in Boston. Look, is there anything else you can tell me? Like I say, I got some experience."

"Sorry. We're just getting started."

A pause. "Okay."

She thanked Fallon, hung up, and told Jeff about the gun.

"Wasn't in the trunk," he said. "Or the glove box—I looked in there, too."

"And it wasn't in her purse or coat, or under the seat."

"Maybe she tried to use it and the perp—or perps—took it away from her. Or it could be here. But then…"

She nodded. If Alicia had left it at home, that might suggest she was less worried about someone she didn't know than someone she did.

She punched in the Bradfords's number and got Susan Bradford. As she explained the situation, Mrs. Bradford interjected tiny cheeps of distress.

"Did she express any concern for her safety?" Cynthia said.

"No. But she's never been terribly open with us. Oh, God."

"Let me give you my number," Cynthia said.

"Wait. I can't find the pen."

"That's all right. Take your time."

"Oh, here it is. Sorry. I'm ready now."

Cynthia spoke the number slowly and repeated it. "If you think of anything," she said, "please call me."

"I'm sure Sam—" Mrs. Bradford's voice broke on her husband's name, "—will want to…"

"Certainly. Thank you."

She hung up and grimaced at Jeff.

Chapter 5

They talked to Alicia's neighbors who were home and learned nothing about her weekend or about her. Two of them didn't even recognize her from the copy of the ID photo. When they were done, they drove to the boarding house of the FBI's person of interest on the chance they'd catch him before he went to work.

She told Jeff about him on the way. "Christopher Mallory. Late-twenties, single, clerks in a shoe store. Arrested for window peeping when he was nineteen. The second victim disappeared from a lot across from the shoe store. She was a CPA, working late, and a witness saw a black car like Mallory's pull out of the lot at about the right time. Also, the FBI found a big collection of bondage porn in his room. But they couldn't nail him. Still, he's what we've got at the moment."

Mallory's street had once been the domain of the second-tier well-to-do, but now it mostly served the residential needs of off-campus students. Its big Victorians had become rooming houses and subdivided, low-rent apartments, and their shabby exteriors reflected their use. But the maples planted along the sidewalks in that earlier time lent the decline a genteel ambience and, at present, a first blush of autumn beauty. A red leaf scuttled across the windshield as they parked.

The house Mallory boarded in was a gray, gabled three-story with a front porch badly in need of paint. Cynthia pressed the buzzer, heard nothing, and rapped on the door. She was about to knock again when a smallish man opened it. He had fluffy white hair, but his smooth face and bright blue eyes made it hard to estimate his age. He could have been anywhere from thirty-five to fifty-five. He wore a pullover sweater of pastel patches, and he was holding a mug with a dunking tag over the side. He smiled at them and said in a light Southern voice, the kind verging on effeminacy, "May I help you?"

She showed him her badge. "We're looking for Chris Mallory."

"Oh, he moved out."

"When?"

"It must be two weeks ago now."

"You know where he went?"

"Chesapeake, he said. "He has a sister there."

"Are you the owner of this house?"

He smiled again. "Yes, but I still can't help thinking of it as Momma's."

"Did Mallory leave a forwarding address?"

"He did. But I don't recall offhand where I put it. Please come in while I have a look."

He led them at a languorous pace past a staircase with a threadbare carpet and down a musty hallway. "I'm Fred Winslow, by the way," he said over his shoulder. "People call me Freddy, I don't know why exactly. I suppose I must look like a Freddy to them."

Near the end of the hall they followed him through a door into a big room, half den and half kitchen. Dirty dishes lay piled in the sink and on the counters, there was an odor of rotting food, and the round table in the center was heaped with letters and newspapers and tools and more dishes. Jeff, a neat freak with the tidiest desk in the division, popped his eyes at her.

"These are my living quarters," Freddy said. He waved his hand toward an inner door. "Our bedrooms are back there—mine and Momma's, or what used to be hers. I'm afraid I've let things slide a little since she passed."

Jeff gave her another look.

Freddy pushed some stuff away from the table edge, knocking over a small mammy figurine in red kerchief and dress, and set his mug down. He picked through the jumble until he found a wooden recipe box. "Might be in here," he said. He opened the box and lifted out pieces of paper one at a time. "No," he said to each of them. He put the box back in the pile and walked over to the refrigerator, where notes were attached by bits of freezer tape. There were so many they gave the door a feathery appearance. "No," he said as he put his finger on each one. He turned around and froze, his eyes going blank, and just as suddenly he came to life again. "It could be in my dresser," he said. "I'll just go and check."

"Take your time," Jeff said.

Freddy disappeared into the back.

Jeff picked up the mammy. "Salt shaker. Uncle Tom must be down there somewhere in the briar patch."

"Or behind you." Cynthia nodded toward a display cabinet full of black figurines.

"Jesus," Jeff said. He walked over to it.

Freddy came back holding a piece of paper. When he saw Jeff by the cabinet, he said, "Momma loved to collect figurines. She was especially fond of little dogs."

"She must've had a soft spot for little pickaninnys, too," Jeff said. "She's got a whole bunch here eating watermelon and another whole bunch sticking out of alligator mouths."

"Yes, those are hard to find," Freddy said without a trace of irony.

He handed Cynthia a piece of paper. "I probably should hold onto that, but I can copy it for you if—"

"That's all right," Cynthia said, whipping out her notebook. "I'll do it." She saw Mallory had provided a phone number.

"I hope Chris isn't in any trouble. He was such a polite young man. He even apologized for the FBI people storming up to his room."

Cynthia had never seen Mallory's room, although she'd spent a few evenings parked outside the house. "Why did he leave?" she said.

"He really didn't say, but I think, you know, it had to do with him being treated like some sort of a criminal. Would you all like some tea?"

"No, thanks," Cynthia said.

"So it'd be hard to find one of those gators eating a black baby?" Jeff said.

"I'm afraid so." Freddy smiled.

"Shame."

They went back to the car and Cynthia called the number. A woman answered.

"Is this Mary Beth Davis?" Cynthia said.

"Yes."

"This is Investigator Westbrook, Harris County sheriff's, Virginia. I need to talk to your brother Christopher."

"Well, you'll have to call the jail. That's where they got him."

"What's he doing in jail?"

"Some girl said he tried to pull her into his car."

"Abduct her, you mean?"

"That's what she says."

"How long has he been in there?"

"Since last Tuesday."

"You have the phone number of the jail?"

Mary Beth Davis gave it to her. She called and confirmed the story. Under the pretense of asking for directions, Mallory had tried to grab a fifteen-year-old walking to a friend's house, but she'd escaped and later identified him in a line-up.

"Can't be our guy," she told Jeff.

"But he coulda been. Maybe he did the first two, and somebody else did the third. I might have to change my mind about the poet."

From Freddy's they drove to the North Hill police station. When they entered the lobby a big man in a wrinkled brown suit rose from one of the chairs and approached them. He had a meaty face with deep grooves around the mouth and pouches under the eyes. She guessed who he was. He must have left Baltimore right after they'd talked.

"Detective Westbrook?" he said. "I'm Fallon."

"Mr. Fallon."

"I went to the sheriff's office, and they said you were still in North Hill."

She caught a whiff of booze on his breath, a bad sign given the time of day and the fact he'd been driving. But he seemed sober enough.

"Jeff White," Jeff said, and shook his hand. "Sorry about your niece. Excuse me, I've gotta check on something."

The lobby was empty, so Cynthia guided him to some chairs in the corner and pulled hers out to face him. Best to keep him away from what Jeff would be doing.

"Nothing much to tell you at this point," she said.

His small black eyes gave her a cop stare. "Just so you know, I plan to stick around. You can reach me here." He gave her a slip of paper with Wayside Inn scrawled on it. The Wayside was a cheap motel west of town that had recently been the scene of a drug death.

Trying to size him up, she said, "You told me you'd lost touch with Alicia. How'd the two of you get reacquainted?"

"Susan, her aunt, called and said she was moving here."

Susan Bradford had been watching out for Alicia, it seemed, even if Alicia hadn't invited the attention. "And you came to see her?"

"Yeah, a few times."

"The accident that killed her family—that happen in Maryland?"

"No, Virginia. That's where they were living."

"Virginia? Whereabouts?"

"Outside a place called Sperryville, not too far south of here."

"I know Sperryville. Sort of artsy."

"Yeah, well, they were both artists—my sister Kathleen and her husband Frank."

"You ever see the pictures in Alicia's bedroom?"

"No."

"There's a painting of a farmhouse and a drawing of two little girls."

"Probably some of theirs. They lived in an old farmhouse, and Kathleen loved to draw. She did it from the time she could hold a pencil. Amazing stuff for a kid. I don't know where she got it from. Our dad never did anything with his hands except pour drinks and make change at his bar, and Ma was a pretty fair singer, but that was the extent of her talent."

"Did Alicia have a younger sister?"

He nodded. "Evie. She was killed in the accident along with Kathleen and Frank. Kathleen had talked to Ma that evening and said Evie had a fever. I guess it got worse and they decided to take her to a hospital. Drunk ran a stoplight and hit 'em broadside. Alicia was in the front with Frank, opposite the impact, but she got pretty busted up. She was in a coma for three days."

"She woke up to no family."

"Yeah. It was tough. First time I saw her here, she told me she'd driven down to see the farmhouse, but it was gone, burned up in a fire. Nothing left but the chimneys. She asked me what I remembered about it, from the couple times I took Ma there. I told her about Frank knocking out a wall to make a big studio, and Kathleen painting the porch floor purple and the swing yellow. I didn't tell her she wouldn't have lived there much longer anyway. Frank, the bastard, was humping some woman in town.

He was going to move in with her, but Kathleen talked him into staying a few more weeks until school was over, and then she was coming back to Baltimore with the kids. That's how it would've played out if Evie hadn't gotten sick."

Childhood's end either way, Cynthia thought.

"I'm slowing you down," he said, and stood up.

She stood up too.

"I'd appreciate it," he said, "if you'd keep me in the loop, in a general way."

"Sure."

They shook hands, cop to cop, and she watched him leave, a big, sad, angry man, and maybe a drunk. She felt sorry for him, but she wasn't sure she trusted him.

She went inside and found Jeff at a back table with a TV. He was drinking coffee and eating a donut from somebody's box on the table.

"How'd it go?" he said.

"Hard to tell. He's hanging around."

"I could call my cousin in Baltimore. He's got a friend on the force."

She thought about it. "Okay. Wouldn't hurt."

"Now, wanna know what I found out?"

"Yep."

"She did buy a gun, last Thursday. A .38 Special just like Uncle Mike recommended." He swiveled his chair toward the TV. "And take a look at this. It's from a camera mounted on the grocery-store ceiling."

He pushed a button on the TV, and a color image of the store entrance appeared. After a few seconds, a young woman in a camel coat and a black knit cap entered.

"That's our vic, isn't it?" he said.

"Yes."

He speeded up the tape, zipping several people in and out the door, and slowed it down again. Alicia left carrying her two bags of groceries. Then he fast-forwarded and slowed, and a man with a single bag in his hand moved toward the door. His back was to the camera, but he wore a patchwork sweater, his hair was white and fluffy, and he strolled along in a familiarly indolent way.

"Looks like Freddy," she said.

"Has to be. Who else would wear that sweater? And check the time. Seven minutes after she paid."

"She could have walked to her car and driven away by then."

"Unless she went in another store, or stopped to talk to somebody, or forgot where she parked."

"Her place and Freddy's are roughly equidistant from the grocery. He'd have as much reason to shop there as she would."

"But there's also his connection to Mallory."

"Who's in jail in Chesapeake."

"For attempted kidnapping. Maybe he and Freddy were working together until the feds put the spotlight on him."

"Hard to imagine Freddy having the wherewithal, or the energy, to kidnap anybody."

"Could be an act to throw us off."

"I don't think his room was an act. But we can give him another look. Right now, though, we need to write those warrants. I'll take Alicia's apartment if you do her office."

Jeff held up the box of donuts. "Eat something first. You're running on fumes."

She realized he was right. She felt hollowed out by exhaustion, scooped into a brittle shell that might crack and disintegrate at any moment. She grabbed a donut and headed toward an empty desk.

Chapter 6

They got the warrants signed in the old courthouse across the street and drove back to Alicia's apartment. The silence there seemed to have thickened since the morning, and the soft light filling the yellow living room curtains no longer felt connected to a specific observer: it was there for anybody, or nobody.

They set aside the laptop and the bills and records she'd neatly filed in a desk drawer and that, at first glance, appeared to be of no consequence. In the top drawer was a small album of faded color photographs. Cynthia recognized the children from the drawing and the farmhouse from the painting. Alicia's parents looked quite young. The mother was thin and blonde, with sharp features, the father handsome but given to making goofy faces for the camera. There were pictures of the sisters in various costumes, Evie mugging like her father but Alicia taking her role seriously, whatever it was. In one she wore the homemade sorcerer's hat and the star quilt.

There was also a photo of a dark-haired Fallon and an older woman, obviously his mother from her strong facial resemblance to the Fallon of today, standing with Kathleen and the girls. The album was the only personal item. There were no journals or letters, although the laptop might have something. No gun, either, but on a closet shelf they found a box of ammo minus a few bullets.

Jeff bagged a hairbrush and toothbrush for the DNA. They put them in the car along with the computer and the records and took them to the evidence room at headquarters. Then they drove to the college and climbed the stairs of Allen Hall to the English offices. She showed the search warrant to Laura, who silently walked them down to Alicia's office and unlocked the door. They shut it behind them and looked around. A picture calendar on the wall showed a black-and-white drawing of a girl peering over a mushroom at a hookah-smoking caterpillar.

"*Alice in Wonderland*," Jeff said.

"Alicia specialized in children's literature."

"Alice and Alicia. Curiouser and curiouser." He grinned at her. "I may be illiterate, but I know my Disney movies."

The date blocks under the picture were blank except for *dept meeting 1 p.m.* written in the next day's space. She flipped the October picture down and saw a similar reminder in September but also, penned beneath Saturday the fifth, *Walt 3 p.m.*

She made a note of it.

"We talking to this guy?" Jeff said.

Cynthia, who'd been watching the time, said, "His class ends in forty minutes."

She checked the next two months, both blank, and went backward from October through the rest of the calendar, finding only work-related notes and other illustrations—a gigantic Alice filling a whole room, the Mad Hatter's tea party, the Cheshire Cat grinning from a tree. After that, they searched the desk and the filing cabinet but found nothing of interest.

With ten minutes to spare, they went to the department office and asked Laura for Lewis's classroom number, in case he left from there. But Laura said she'd seen him going to his office. They walked back down the hall and knocked on his door.

A youngish man answered the knock. He looked grim.

"Are you the detectives?" he said.

She introduced herself and Jeff. "We'd like to ask you some questions," she said.

"Of course." His Adam's apple bobbed in his thick neck. "I hope—I don't know what I hope. That this is some sort of a mistake, I guess."

He moved aside and they entered. Gesturing at the one extra chair, he said, "There's... if anyone would like to sit."

"That's okay," Jeff said, closing the door.

She wouldn't have taken him for a poet, although she knew they came in all shapes and sizes. He had a snub nose, a long jaw, and deep-set brown eyes. His light brown hair was cut short. He wore a corduroy sports coat over a green T-shirt, a pair of worn jeans, and loafers.

"When did you last see her?" Cynthia said.

"Friday afternoon. She came by my office."

"Why?"

"She—she wanted to know my opinion of a poem."

"You talk about anything else?"

"No."

"Did she seem worried or frightened?"

He shook his head.

"Did you know she'd recently purchased a gun?"

"A gun? No. Why?"

"We're trying to find out. How would you describe your relationship with her?"

His Adam's apple bobbed again. "Collegial. Friendly."

Remembering what Laura had told her, Cynthia said, "The two of you see much of each other?"

"We'd chat if we ran into each other in the halls. And sometimes she'd drop by my office."

"No contact outside of the college?"

"No."

An error or a lie, assuming they'd kept their Saturday date. But she decided not to pursue that just yet. "Thanks for your time," she said.

"Do you have any idea who…" he said.

"We're just beginning our investigation."

In the stairwell, Jeff said to her, "I don't know if he offed her, but I'll bet he boffed her."

"*Offed* and *boffed*—that's a near rhyme," she said. "Unlike *moon* and *June*."

"Near rhyme, huh? Must be what lazy poets use, unless they're really lazy like Milton."

Roger called and said he was on his way to the shopping center with four other detectives. Cynthia and Jeff met them there and filled them in. Roger listened in glum, gum-chewing silence. Not a good sign, Cynthia thought. He would have looked happier if the case had gone to her and Jeff. After he heard their report, he passed around some fliers with a fuzzy four by six inch enlargement of an ID photo and the relevant information: name and physical description, place last seen, and a tip number. The team spread out, and two hours later, having interviewed the employees at the grocery and the other stores, they'd come up with zilch. A couple of grocery workers remembered seeing Alicia, but that was all. No one remembered anyone following her or staring at her. Several, however, did recall Freddy, whom Jeff made a point of asking about. He was a regular. Pug-nosed Christine, happy to see Jeff again, went on about Freddy at some length. "He used to come in with his mom," she said. "She was a pretty lady, and very sweet to everybody. But she treated him like a servant. He'd push the cart around, and she'd point to things and he'd get them. And he always brought the car up for her, even when the weather was nice. Now when he comes in, he wanders around forever, but he doesn't buy very much. And if you're checking him out, he'll tell you the whole plot of some movie he's seen. He loves movies. Sometimes I'll say I've seen it even if I haven't, so he'll stop talking and I can check the next person."

As they walked back to the car, Cynthia stopped and looked at the lighted storefronts and the dark tree shapes behind them.

"Déjà vu all over again," Jeff said.

"Still want to take a run at Freddy?"

"I'd like to see what he says about last night."

Three college-age kids, two boys and a girl, were sitting on Freddy's front porch in plastic chairs. Despite the chill they wore only T-shirts and shorts. Insulated by their youth, Cynthia supposed, and maybe by the beer they were drinking.

"Freddy around?" Jeff said.

"I saw him driving off," the girl said.

"When was that?"

"About an hour ago."

"Know where he was going?"

"Nope. Are you guys, like, cops?"

"Maybe they're with the department of mental health," one of the boys said.

"Or the wuss patrol," the other boy said, and the three of them laughed giddily.

"Doesn't seem fair, does it?" Jeff said. "You can vote at eighteen but you gotta be twenty-one to drink."

That gave them pause, and Cynthia said to the girl, "We're sheriff's investigators. Ever have any trouble with Mr. Winslow?"

"Trouble? You mean like sex stuff?"

One of the boys giggled and shut himself up.

"Anything."

"No, not Freddy. There was this guy who lived here. I heard he'd been in some sort of trouble with the FBI. He was always offering to drive me places, but he moved out."

"You ever go with him?" Jeff said.

"No, sir."

"Good decision. He's in jail now for attempted kidnapping."

They returned to the car to wait for Freddy. He showed up an hour and a half later, and Cynthia got out and invited him to join her on the back seat.

When she climbed in beside him, he said, "I was at the Cineplex. Movies are my vice."

Volunteered information always roused her suspicion. "What did you see?" she said.

"A horror movie about this girl with a curse on her. She works in a bank and this old woman comes in to ask for a loan, and she—"

"That's okay," Cynthia said. "We were wondering if you could help us with something."

"Surely. If I can."

"Have you heard about the woman who went missing last night?"

He nodded. "It was on the car radio just now."

"Did they say where she disappeared from?"

"Yes. Greenwood Shopping Center."

"That's not too far from here, is it? You ever shop there?"

"Yes."

"How about last night?"

"Yes, I believe so."

"In fact, you were in the grocery store at the same time she was. We have you on the surveillance video."

She stared at Freddy in the dimness, and he stared blandly back.

"Why didn't you mention that when I asked you about her?"

Freddy shrugged. "Didn't think to, I guess."

"You weren't trying to hide it from me, were you?"

"No, ma'am."

She switched on the overhead light and handed him one of the fliers. He studied it with interest.

"Remember seeing her?" she said. "She was wearing a black knit hat and a camel coat."

Still looking intently, he shook his head.

"Any thoughts on who might have abducted her?"

"Well, it must be the same person who took the other ladies."

She went with his assumption of one person. "He must be pretty clever, wouldn't you say?"

"He could be. But the Green River Killer wasn't very bright, and he didn't get caught for years and years."

"How come you're interested in the Green River Killer?"

"I'm not, particularly. It's just something Chris told me."

"Christopher Mallory? Your boarder?"

"Uh-huh."

"Why would he do that?"

"We were talking, you know, about the missing ladies—not this last one, but the others."

"Did the two of you talk about them a lot?"

"No. Only that one time, right after the second lady disappeared."

"But you did talk. You were friends."

"I wouldn't say so, no. We didn't talk very much."

"He ever show you his magazines?"

"What magazines?"

"Ones with pictures of women tied up, being hurt."

"Are you sure you mean Chris? He was such a nice young man."

"He just got arrested in Chesapeake for trying to kidnap a girl."

"He did?"

"He ever suggest that the two of you might enjoy doing something like that together?"

"Oh, no."

"But it's an exciting idea, isn't it? In a movie kind of way."

"Movies aren't real life," Freddy said.

"But you wish they were."

"I like to go to the movies, that's all."

She left it there, unsatisfactorily, and they watched him amble up the steps of the now empty porch.

"Weirder and weirder," Jeff said.

"Yeah. Let's see if his story checks out."

They drove to the Cineplex and indeed Freddy had been there; he was well known to the teenaged staff. One of them referred to him as "that strange little dude."

Outside in the parking lot, Jeff said, "Did you smell that popcorn?"

"Yeah."

"Remind you of anything?"

"Like what?"

"I don't know. Food, maybe."

"You saying you're hungry?"

"That stale cop donut is getting lonely."

She drove them to a hamburger stand she knew, and while they were eating in the car, she called Walter Lewis's home number.

"Hello," a woman said. Children were yelling in the background.

"May I speak to Walter Lewis?"

"Hold on, please."

The woman's voice mingled with the children's, and the yelling stopped. A few more seconds passed and Walter Lewis said, "Hello?" He sounded out of breath.

"Investigator Westbrook, Mr. Lewis. You okay?"

"Pardon me? Oh, sorry. I was exercising."

"I was wondering if you could come to the sheriff's office tomorrow morning. We'd like to ask you a few more questions."

"I could, but I'm afraid I don't know anything else."

"You might without realizing it. It works that way sometimes."

"All right, then. Whatever I can do to help."

She asked where he lived, gave him the directions, and hung up.

Leaning her head against the rest, she gazed at the dark field beyond the parking lot.

"Think it's still our case?" Jeff said.

"Don't know. The signs aren't favorable."

"Roger?"

"Yeah."

"Maybe if we keep juking and jiving."

"Maybe." She closed her eyes.

"Want me to drive?"

"No, I'm good."

"Of course you are."

His mild sarcasm registered after his voice did, like a faint echo. She felt herself teetering on the brink of sleep, and the instant before she forced her eyes open she saw Alicia, the grown-up version in the knit cap, standing under a tree with the star quilt pulled around her.

Chapter 7

She arrived at the station early enough to look through Alicia's things from the car and the apartment. Since the laptop hadn't been hacked yet, the cell phone was the obvious starting point. She accessed its history and found no calls either way on the weekend of the disappearance. Over the last few months there were calls from the Bradfords and Mike Fallon as well as Alicia's recent one to him, when she must have asked about a gun, but none to or from Walter Lewis's office and home numbers. Jeff came in while she was doing this and dumped the contents of Alicia's purse on the table. He picked up the memo pad and flipped it open.

"The top sheet has some indentations," he said, "but not enough for a grocery list. Or a two-bags-full one, anyway."

"Got a number two pencil?"

"I'll steal one from the desk."

He left and returned with a pencil. She rubbed it softly across the indentations until a white scrawl appeared.

"Nine, twenty-seven, two," she read aloud. "What's the first thing?"

"Han? No, B-a-n-something. Bank?"

"A bank appointment two weeks ago, at two o'clock?"

Jeff rifled through the boxed records. "She's got statements from Southland."

"We could try the branch nearest her apartment."

They examined the rest of the stuff, making no discoveries, and went up to their floor to await Walter Lewis. He arrived promptly at the agreed-upon time. Cynthia ushered him into an interrogation room and told him she'd be with him in a moment. She joined Jeff in another room where they could watch him on a monitor. Lewis surveyed his dull surroundings with jerky head movements, then took out a notebook and a pen and began to write.

"What's he doing?" Jeff said. "Composing a poem?"

"Whatever it is, it's calming him down. We don't need that."

She went in, apologized for the delay, and asked what he was writing.

"Just some thoughts," he said, and put the notebook away.

"Thoughts about this place?"

"No, not directly."

She let it go. She wanted to unsettle him, and she doubted that asking him about his work would accomplish that. "Did you remember anything that might help us?" she said.

"No, I'm sorry."

"What was it again you and Ms. Bradford talked about on Friday?"

"She asked my opinion of a poem."

"Which?" she said quickly, to see if she could catch him having to invent something.

Surprised, he said, "'Directive,' by Robert Frost."

"You didn't discuss anything else?"

"No."

"Your other conversations with her—what were they like?"

"They were similar. We talked about literature mostly, or college matters."

"Nothing personal?"

He swallowed and looked away. "No."

"Excuse me, Mr. Lewis, but I find that a little hard to believe. The two of you were friendly, she came to your office a number of times, and the talk never got even a little bit personal?"

He shook his head.

"You did notice she was pretty."

"Yes."

"You ever see her outside the college?"

"No."

She made a show of flipping through her notebook. "Then what about this reminder in her calendar: Walt, three p.m.?"

"I don't know…"

"It's for Saturday, September 5."

"Oh. My wife and I gave a dinner party for the department, and Alicia came. But we really didn't talk much at the party."

Not what she'd anticipated, but she needed to stay on the offensive. "Others can confirm the dinner?"

"Yes, almost everybody in the—why? Surely you don't think I had anything to do with…"

"Could you tell me where you were Sunday evening?"

Now he looked distinctly uneasy. "I took a drive."

"Where to?"

"To my office at the college."

"You drove into North Hill?"

"Yes."

"Why?"

"I needed a place where I could concentrate."

"What time did you get there?"

"I'm not sure. I left home after dinner, around six-thirty."

He'd told her on the phone that he lived on Mount Zion Road midway between Parkerville and Calvary. From there he could have driven to North Hill via two routes: north to Parkerville and west on 7, or southwest to Calvary and northwest on 734. The distances were about the same, twenty to twenty-five miles. Either way, he could have reached North Hill by seven or shortly thereafter, giving him time to intercept Alicia after she left the grocery store at 7:41.

"How long were you in your office?" she said.

"Not very long, a few minutes. I changed my mind and drove home."

The change of mind invited exploration, but she wanted to get a handle on the time line first. "When did you arrive back at your house?"

"A little after nine."

"It took you that long to get home?"

"I stopped at a roadhouse on the way."

Only one place along his possible routes fit this description. "Gilley's?"

"Yes, I think so."

"When'd you get there?"

"I'm not sure."

"How long did you stay?"

"An hour, maybe."

Assuming the times he'd given her were accurate, everything depended on the times he'd been vague about. A matter of minutes could be crucial. She decided not to press him until she had more information. Besides, she wanted to attack on another front. She wrote down his answers regarding the evening slowly, in order to make him nervous. Then she looked him in the eye and said, "You're a poet, Mr. Lewis. You have a good imagination. So I'm sure you can imagine what I'm thinking."

"No," he said. "I have no idea."

"An attractive woman lures a married man into an affair. He comes to his senses and tries to end it. She threatens to tell his wife, or maybe she says she's pregnant."

"Nothing like that ever happened," he said.

"You're denying you had sex with her?"

"I'm not denying it. I'm saying it didn't happen."

"So we won't find witnesses or motel receipts that tell a different story."

His face flushed. "Look," he said in a shaky voice, "I came here for Alicia, and I've answered your questions. Am I free to go?"

"It's in your interest to cooperate, Mr. Lewis."

"I'll take that as a yes," he said, and stood up.

Modulating her tone between an order and a request, she said, "Please sit down."

He moved to the door, opened it, and walked out.

Jeff was waiting for her in the room with the monitor.

"Temper, temper," he said. "You struck something."

"Yeah," she said. "But what?"

Chapter 8

Just beyond the turn onto Mount Zion, they passed an Episcopal church with a little cemetery, and Cynthia thought of Bill, gone six years this November. She'd shared his cabin on Sally's horse farm when she'd worked there, and since he had no family, Sally had buried him in the hilltop cemetery of the property's previous owners. A dozen headstones inside a low wrought-iron fence, the cemetery would have remained half-buried beneath weeds and briars if Bill hadn't made its upkeep a personal duty. "I don't think those folks will mind his company," Sally had said to her. "He's been communing with them for years."

Communing through his hands, Cynthia thought. Bill's hands—pecan brown on top and paler underneath, the fingers long and the knuckles arthritically enlarged—had always been in motion, grooming and soothing horses, caressing vegetables in his garden, pulling weeds, polishing his car, rolling out biscuit dough, jumping checkers on the checkerboard. A wave of sadness rolled through her. She'd assumed she was past grieving, but apparently not.

Jeff pointed out a house on the left. "Walt's place," he said.

She looked at it as they went by. A big Dutch Colonial in a semi-rural setting, with a wide front yard and woods behind.

"By the way," he said, "I called my cousin's buddy on the Baltimore police."

"Learn anything?"

"He didn't know Fallon, but he'd heard of him. Couple years back

Fallon wrestled a guy down who'd pulled a gun on his ex-wife—the guy's ex-wife. She was a barmaid, and Fallon happened to be in the bar. He took a bullet in the chest."

"Brave man."

"Yeah. And if he was a booze hound, the buddy didn't know about it."

Not far past the Lewises the sense of a middle-class suburb disappeared. On one side of the road was fenced pastureland; on the other, shallow fields being swallowed up by the woods that ran behind the Lewis home—protected forest, she knew, jointly owned by the state and a conservation group. Nearer Calvary, ramshackle houses and rusty trailers occupied the forest apron, a fitting prelude to the town. They drove through its bleak heart and headed northwest on 734 to Gilley's, a no-frills roadhouse with a painted sign over the door and a gravel parking lot. Not the sort of place that Walter Lewis would frequent, she imagined. He probably wasn't dissembling when he seemed unsure of its name.

They parked and went in. At eleven-thirty in the morning there were no customers. A hefty woman in jeans and a T-shirt was wiping a tabletop in a booth. Behind the bar a pale, cadaverous man stood sipping a cup of coffee.

Jeff showed the man his badge and asked if he'd been working on Sunday evening.

"I work every evening," the man said. "I'm Gilley."

"You remember a guy that night," Jeff said, "early to mid-thirties, brown hair, medium build? My guess is he'd be the only one without a padded vest and a ball cap."

Gilley said to the woman, "There was somebody like that, wasn't there, Rhonda?"

"Yeah, he set over there," the woman said, pointing to an end booth.

"When'd he come in?" Jeff said.

"Seven-thirty or eight," the woman said.

"Which is it?"

Rhonda shrugged.

"You can't be more specific?"

"Not unless you want me to lie. Tell me what he done, and I might could."

"I appreciate your public spirit, but no thanks." Jeff looked at Gilley. "You remember when he came in?"

Gilley shook his head.

"How'd he pay?" Cynthia asked.

"I do remember that," Rhonda said. "Cash. And he left a big ole quarter tip."

"Other than the fact he was a cheapskate," Jeff said, "you notice anything else?"

"There was one funny thing. He nursed his drink awhile, and then he got up and stood in front of the phone." She nodded toward the pay phone on the end wall behind her. "But he never did call nobody. Just stared at it and set back down again and nursed his drink some more."

When they got in the car, Jeff said, "It's, what, seven, eight miles to North Hill from here?"

"About that."

"If he stopped here on his way home *around* eight, meaning a few minutes after, he could've abducted and killed the vic at a quarter of and made it this far. No time to dump the body, but he could've done it afterward."

"Suppose he got here a few minutes before eight."

"Then we're screwed. We need to talk to those Sunday customers."

"We probably just talked to the two most sober people in the place that night."

"Good point. What about the phone thing? Who do you think it was he didn't call?"

She shook her head.

"If he showed after eight," Jeff said, "maybe it was the police. Maybe he was trying to work up the nerve to turn himself in."

"If and maybe."

"Just throwing it out there."

"I know, but let's not go chasing it yet."

Her cell rang. It was Roger. She gave him a brief update, leaving out the imponderables.

"Okay, thanks," he said. "Sampson's holding a news conference at three in North Hill, on the courthouse steps. He wants you there."

She hung up and told Jeff.

"Sampson wants us," he said. "Might be a good sign."

Judging by the gloom in Roger's voice, she didn't think so, but it was possible they'd remain the de facto lead, which would be all right with her.

"Why don't we talk to Mrs. Lewis," she said. "Alicia's calendar showed a department meeting today at one. Walter Lewis will be there, I assume."

Jeff glanced at his watch. "That give us time to eat first?"

"Yeah, if you want."

"Want? Eating isn't, you know, like a hobby. It's not like knitting or stamp collecting. You have to do it every now and then."

They drove back into Calvary. The restaurant she remembered, the only one, had gone out of business, but there was a little Hispanic grocery with a string of plastic chili peppers in the window. They bought some tamales wrapped in cornhusks and kept warm in a big metal pot, a bag of tortilla chips, and cans of soda. Jeff also got himself a Twinkie. They climbed back in the car with their lunch and spread the old newspaper sheets they'd been given on their laps.

"I didn't know you liked Twinkies," she said.

He looked at her. "What's wrong with Twinkies?"

"Nothing. It's just that I haven't had any since I was a kid."

"You were a kid?"

"Once upon a time."

"Might be good to keep that in mind."

He made something of a show of enjoying his Twinkie, and then they went to the Lewises.

Mrs. Lewis answered the doorbell with a little blonde girl on her hip and a boy of three or four standing close beside her. She was dressed in jeans and a faded orange sweatshirt. She had blonde hair like her daughter, and a sturdy, strong-featured face. Her sleeves were speckled with what looked like dried mud.

Cynthia introduced herself and Jeff.

"Are you the ones Walt talked to?" Mrs. Lewis said.

"That's right. May we come in?"

"Sure." She held out a dirty sleeve. "Excuse the grunge. I was throwing a pot."

Nothing in her manner, Cynthia thought, suggested that she knew about the thrust of the interview with her husband. "You're a potter?" she said.

"Yes. I'm just getting back to it after the move."

She led them into a sunny living room with a view of the woods. The little girl, refusing to be put down, nestled in her mother's lap and looked shyly askance at them. The boy sat beside his mother on the couch, his skinny legs and sneakers straight out in front of him.

"I understand Alicia Bradford attended your dinner party in September," Cynthia said.

"Yes. It's still hard to believe…" She glanced at her children.

Cynthia nodded. "How well did you know her?"

"I didn't know her at all, really. It was the only time we met."

"What was your impression of her?"

"Serious. A little lonely. But she seemed to enjoy the kids. We have another boy who's in school, and—"

"Tommy," the little girl blurted.

"Yes," her mother said. "Tommy's in second grade. And this is Amy, and that's Bobby. The lady who works with Daddy played with you, didn't she?"

"We played catch," Bobby said. "But Amy's too little so the lady had to roll her the ball."

Cynthia smiled at him and said to Mrs. Lewis, "She didn't seem worried or agitated?"

"No. Why? You don't think she knew—"

"Knew what, Mommy?" Bobby said.

"Nothing, honey."

"Hey, where's that ball?" Jeff said. "I'd like to play some catch, too."

Tommy looked eagerly at his mother, who said to him, "It's okay. Go get it." He raced out of the room and came back with the ball. Jeff took the kids outside where Mrs. Lewis could see them through the window. She and Cynthia watched as he hoisted Amy on his shoulders and handed her the ball.

"He seems nice," Mrs. Lewis said.

"He has his moments. To answer your question, we don't think anything yet. We're just exploring the possibilities."

Her eye still on Jeff and the children, Mrs. Lewis said, "We didn't hear about the women until the second one disappeared. By then, Walt had accepted the job, but even if he hadn't I would have wanted him to. It's a tenured position. His other offer was a one-year writer in residence, and there've been too many of those. All the moving around hasn't been good for the kids. Plus I'd found this house—it's the nicest one we've ever had. We're even renting with the option to buy, which is a first for us. But now I don't know. Alicia's disappearance brings it all so close."

Cynthia had been pondering whether to bring up Walter's Sunday drive. His departure and arrival times weren't at issue, since they didn't give him an alibi. But Mrs. Lewis appeared not to have connected the drive to Alicia's abduction, and asking her about it might elicit something. On the other hand, the threat of connecting the dots, which their visit underscored, might induce Walter to talk to them again. She decided on an indirect approach for now. Next to the hearth was a large green vase, tapered at both ends with a sort of embossed surface. She pointed to it and said, "Is that one of yours?"

"Yes."

"Very nice."

"Thanks."

"How does it work, being a mother and a potter?"

"It doesn't, sometimes. But that's okay. I was the one who wanted a family."

Some tension there, Cynthia thought. She remembered the kids yelling in the background when Mrs. Lewis answered the phone, and Walter coming on out of breath from exercise. He'd left the child watching up to her. And there was Bobby's eagerness to play with Jeff. Whatever else Walter was, he didn't seem to be much of a father.

"Thanks for your time," she said.

"You know what went through my mind when I heard about Alicia?" Mrs. Lewis said. "It happened to her because she was pretty, and so I was safe. Isn't that terrible?"

Was she hinting that she suspected an affair, or was this something bubbling up from the unconscious?

"You said she seemed lonely," Cynthia said, "but do you think she might have been seeing someone when she disappeared?"

"I don't know. I don't know anything about her."

"Okay. Thanks." Cynthia made eye contact with her. "Your reaction to the news wasn't terrible; it was human. And you do need to stay cautious."

As they drove away, Jeff said, "Walt didn't tell her you grilled him, did he?"

"Nope."

"You ask her about Sunday evening?"

"Not yet. Learn anything from the kids?"

"They said Daddy left that evening because they were noisy. Daddy doesn't like noise."

"Figures. She told me the kids were her idea."

"Wife who wants kids who spoil your concentration. Pretty good rationalization for some extra-curricular boffing."

"Yeah," she said, "but not for an offing."

Chapter 9

They arrived in north hill fifty minutes ahead of the news conference. Not wanting to waste any opportunity to stake their claim, they located the Southland branch nearest Alicia's apartment. When they entered, Jeff spied a pretty African-American teller without a customer and made a beeline for her. He told her about the September twenty-seventh appointment, and she suggested they talk to Mr. Middleton, the chief financial officer.

"Thank you, Ms., ah…" he said.

"Johnson."

"Here's my card, Ms. Johnson, in case you ever need police assistance."

"Thank you, Mr. White," she said, looking at the card. "I hope I won't."

"But if you do, I'll be happy to help."

They walked over to Middleton's glass-walled, jalousied office and Cynthia rapped on the open door.

The banker swiveled from a side desk, where he'd been gazing at a computer, and invited them to sit down. After Cynthia explained their purpose, he said, "Yes, I remember seeing a young lady around that time. Let me just access my notes." He turned back to the computer and brought up a new screen. "Here it is. Alicia Bradford."

"Why'd she make the appointment?" Cynthia said.

"To see about a home loan. It was a preliminary conversation. I asked her to describe her financial situation and the general condition of the house. My notes say it was an older, unoccupied house. Based on what she told me, I suggested there could be some major additional expenses. Anyway, that was that. I gave her the appropriate forms to fill out, but she didn't follow up. Frankly, it wasn't in her interest to do so."

Thinking that Alicia might also have spoken to the owner or a realtor, Cynthia said, "Do you have the address for the house?"

"Yes, 64 Mount Zion Road."

She and Jeff exchanged glances. The Lewises lived at 52.

"Did she say why she was interested in it?" Cynthia said.

"No, not that I recall. Is Ms. Bradford in some sort of trouble?"

"She's missing."

"Oh. Is she the young lady in the news? I'm so sorry."

Cynthia thanked him, and he rose and offered his hand. "You're quite welcome," he said, giving her a firm handshake. "Good luck with your investigation."

*****

The crowd on the courthouse lawn appeared to consist mostly of reporters and their crews. Cynthia, searching for a parking place, saw a woman she knew from the Parkerville Courier and several over-dressed men and women near big cameras, one with a CNN logo. Above them in the shadow of the portico stood Sampson's group. She found a spot two blocks away, and they walked back and climbed the stone steps. Bunched around Sampson were Roger, Mike Fallon, the North Hill police chief, and a well-groomed couple in their sixties—Alicia's aunt and uncle, she assumed. Both of them wore the blank, stunned expressions of those overtaken by calamity. The man was holding a framed photo of Alicia.

Sampson introduced the couple to them, confirming her guess. "I think you know Mr. Fallon," he said.

"Yeah, we've met," Fallon said. His suit was pressed, and his breath was booze free.

"We'll start in a few minutes," Sampson said. He turned toward Roger and the police chief.

Cynthia said to Susan Bradford, "We spoke on the phone."

"Oh, yes."

"You told me that Alicia wasn't very open with you."

"No."

"Why was that, if you don't mind my asking?"

"It's difficult to—do you know about the accident?"

Cynthia nodded. "Mr. Fallon told me."

"We felt it was our duty to take care of her. Mike wasn't able to, and it was either us or his mother, who was getting on in years. But we hadn't planned on having children. So it was…"

"An adjustment for all of us," Sam Bradford finished for her.

"Our life in the city, everything, was so different from what she was used to. It's understandable she always held back a little."

"But we loved her like our own," Bradford said, and for an instant his pain shone nakedly in his face.

Mrs. Bradford, her eyes glistening, squeezed his arm. "We wanted to adopt her, but she didn't like the idea. I think she saw it as being disloyal to the memory of her parents and her sister. Not that she was unkind about it. She was always such a polite girl. She just said she'd rather leave things as they were, and anyway we already had the same last name."

A couple who hadn't wanted a child, Cynthia thought, had fallen in love with a child who hadn't wanted them. The irony heightened the tragedy. "In your conversations with her," she said, "did she mention any relationship troubles?"

"No," Bradford said. "But we've already gone over that with a detective."

Another sign they'd lost the lead. She looked at Roger, who was spitting gum into a foil wrapper. His eyes darted her way, but he pretended not to see her.

"Did Alicia say anything about buying a house?" she asked.

Bradford's eyebrows shot up. "Was she thinking about buying one?"

"She talked to a loan officer at her bank."

"We could have helped her with that," Mrs. Bradford said, a tear slipping down her delicately rouged cheek. "Why didn't she come to us?"

Sampson turned back to them. "It's time," he said.

They followed him down to the microphone on one of the lower steps. He gave his audience a moment to admire his square-jawed good looks and athletic physique, shown to nice effect in a tailored brown uniform. Then he said, "Good afternoon. I'm Major Harold Sampson of the county sheriff's office, Crimes Against Persons division. As you know, Alicia Bradford, a teacher at Mary Weaver College, went missing on Sunday evening. We have reason to believe she was abducted, and we are devoting all available resources to finding her and apprehending the individual or individuals responsible for her abduction. With me today are Ms. Bradford's aunt and uncle, Susan and Samuel Bradford of Boston; another uncle, Michael Fallon of Baltimore; Chief James Wagner of the North Hill police department; and some of our investigative team, including our team leader Lieutenant Roger Bullock."

Jeff looked at her and mouthed, "Fuck."

"Lieutenant Bullock will now brief you and take any questions," Sampson said.

Roger, a pudgy, heavy-breathing man with a pendulous lower lip, gravely took Sampson's place. While he laid out the basic facts, Cynthia scanned his audience. Killers sometimes attended the public events they caused, which was the reason for the plainclothes photographer circling the crowd's perimeter and taking snaps. A face might connect to something later on. She started her own inspection at the front looking for anyone she'd met in the course of this investigation or the previous ones, and her eye fell on Freddy. He was staring at Roger with a little smile on his face, or maybe a sun squint. She nudged Jeff and whispered, "Right side, near the front."

"Uh huh," he said.

Roger finished his summary and was immediately barraged with requests for details he couldn't divulge. "I can't comment on that," he kept saying until Sampson reclaimed the microphone and announced that Mr. Bradford would speak. Bradford stepped forward and held up the picture.

"This is my niece," he said. "When she was ten years old, her parents and her sister were taken from her in an automobile accident that nearly ended her own life. To whoever is holding her"—*his saving fiction*, Cynthia thought—"I ask you to imagine what she's already been through and show compassion. Please, let her go. To Major Sampson and the local authorities, I want to express our gratitude for the intensive effort now underway. As part of that effort, my wife and I are offering a $200,000 reward for information leading to Alicia's safe return." He paused, his narrow, gray-suited frame erect, a light breeze ruffling his sparse gray hair. "Alicia, dear," he said in a harsh voice, "if you can hear me, we love you and we hope that very soon you'll be safe with us."

When it became clear he'd stopped talking, the reporters pounced on him, asking about his last contact with Alicia and the details of her childhood tragedy. Sampson, to his credit, moved Bradford quickly out of harm's way. "We appreciate you folks spreading the word," Sampson said. "Please take a flier if you don't have one. Our tip number is at the bottom." He read the number aloud. "Also, I'd like to announce that

I requested the assistance of the FBI, and they've loaned us their top profiler, a forensic psychologist."

A profiler and an airtight confession, the saying went, would close a case every time. Not much help there. Sampson was either trying to lure the feds further in, or preparing to spread the blame, if it came to that. Or both. She wondered how she and Jeff figured into his calculations.

"We'll go back up and wait until the press leaves," Sampson told the group.

"Sir," she said, "can I have a word with you?"

Irritation flashed across his face. "Make it brief."

They moved up and away from the microphone. Aware that her greater height annoyed him, she slipped to the step below his.

"My partner and I have been going full tilt on this," she said, "and we hope to keep at it."

"I appreciate your commitment, Westbrook, but what I need from everyone now is commitment to the team. Can I count on you for that?"

"Yes, sir."

"Good. I want you and White to meet with the profiler tomorrow. Two o'clock at the FBI Academy in Quantico."

"With all due respect," Cynthia said, "I believe we'd serve the team better in the field."

"You have a solid lead?"

"We're exploring some possibilities."

"That's what I thought. Okay, Westbrook, you've had your say. And you've got your orders."

They climbed the steps together in silence, Cynthia making sure to stay on a level with him. Jeff was waiting for her at a remove from the others. When she joined him, he said, "Didn't know you were gonna do that."

"Neither did I."

"What's the verdict?"

"We're seeing the profiler tomorrow."

"Double fuck."

Roger came over to them and sheepishly handed her a piece of paper with the profiler's name and phone and fax numbers. "I've already faxed him the other two cases," he said. "Be good if you could send him a report on this one tonight. And the tip line'll probably be going crazy, so I'll need you guys to do a shift tomorrow morning, before you go."

"Want us to clean the bathrooms too?" Jeff said.

Roger gave him a murderous look. "Number one," he said in a fierce whisper, "you're the junior prick in this division. You haven't done shit yet. And B, if it was up to me you could bust your balls on this fucking case till the end of time. But it isn't, so we're all gonna have to suck it up."

"*One* and B don't go together," Jeff said.

"What?"

"It's either *one* and *two*, or *A* and *B*."

"Fuck you," Roger said, and stormed off.

"That was helpful," Cynthia said.

"Oh, you can fix it. He's your puppy dog."

By this point the crowd had dispersed, and they all started down. Fallon, catching up with her and Jeff, said, "How about a cup of coffee? There's a café just up the street."

She started to say they had a report to write, but the loss of the case had taken the wind out of her sails. "All right, I guess we've got a few minutes."

"You two go on," Jeff said. "I need to make a call."

He started off in the direction of the car, and they walked the other way to the café. They ordered at the counter and took their cups to a table. Stirring his coffee to cool it, Fallon said, "How far out they push you?"

"All the way. We're going to Quantico tomorrow."

He grimaced. "Stupid. You're a good cop. I could tell that the first time we talked."

She waited to see whether his flattery had an ulterior motive.

"But you can still show the bastards," he said. "Wherever they stick you, you'll hear things. You can pass them along to me, and I'll do the legwork."

She shook her head. "You know as well as I do that's a bad idea. For Alicia's sake, if nothing else. We'd risk jeopardizing the case."

"I'd never let that happen. I'd ice the son of a bitch first."

"Not your best counter-argument."

He glanced at her bare left hand. "Not married?"

"No."

"Ever been?"

"No."

"I was, twice. Both of 'em hated being a cop's wife. The garbage you don't talk about and they don't want to hear about, the night shifts, the missed dinners, the days you don't come home at all. The first one split after seven years, the second one after three. But I rolled with it. The job kept me going. Then a couple years ago I got shot, and it started me thinking. And where I came out was I'd blown it. No wife and no kids. My parents and sister gone. Alicia was basically it, and I hadn't seen her in years. All I had was the fucking job. So I quit. I'd done some sheet metal work as a kid, and I got back into that with no problem. But it didn't really change anything. Made it worse, in fact. The guys I worked with either went home to their families, or they were loners and drunks. Then Susan called about Alicia moving here, and I got in touch with her. She wasn't all that thrilled to hear from me, but she was a nice girl. She put up with me calling her, and driving over a few times—not enough to get on her nerves, I hoped. It was a start."

"I'm sorry, Mike," she said.

"Yeah."

She took a few sips of her coffee and left him there. On the sidewalk she glanced through the window and saw him tipping a flask into his cup.

Jeff was leaning against the car talking on his cell, but he rang off before she reached him.

"A certain bank teller?" she said.

"Yep."

"Fast work."

"Just trying to get something out of this rotten day."

"Save some part of the day you'd rued."

"Come again?"

"Nothing. It's from a poem. Did you succeed?"

He grinned.

Chapter 10

Roger had been right about the tip line. By the time she and Jeff took over, 213 tips had come in, and they collected another twenty-seven during their shift. The vast majority were off-the-wall theories, with alien abduction leading the pack, offered by people who lived elsewhere, like California, but who had seen the press conference on cable news. There were also the clues of self-identified psychics, visions of things like a plaid hat, the letter M, and a scummy pond. Only two of the most recent tips seemed worth investigating: possible sightings of Alicia at a gas station east of North Hill and on the main street of Calvary. Since these came in late, she and Jeff held onto them. When they finished at eleven, they went to see Roger, who was sulking at his desk.

"Hey, man, I'm sorry about yesterday," Jeff said. "I was just pissed. I know it wasn't your decision."

"That goes for me, too," she said.

"You didn't do anything," Roger said to her. There might be some truth to Jeff's joke that Roger had a crush on her. He often showed up at the coffee table when she was getting a cup and passed by her desk more times than seemed coincidental, even granting that they worked in the same division.

"You're absolutely right," Jeff said to him. "It was all my bad. How are the wife and kids, by the way?"

"Huh?" Roger said.

Judging that Jeff would only make it worse, she quickly mentioned the two sightings and said they could look into them before going to Quantico. Roger gave her the go ahead, and they went down to the parking lot.

"You think Roger's interested in Walter and Freddy?" she said.

"Nope."

"You still interested?"

"Yep."

"Then why don't you talk to Freddy again and maybe track down some of Walter's students. I can go to Quantico by myself."

"Is this your devious way of getting me to say, gee, you're so nice, why don't *you* do the good stuff?"

"No. I was thinking you might have more success with Freddy than I did. And I know you'll do better with the female students, who are the ones to see. But we could split the tips. You take North Hill and I'll take Calvary—it's not far off my route. And while I'm at it, I'll look at that house Alicia thought about buying. See if it has a for sale sign with a name on it."

"Whatever you say, pard."

She took the cop car and drove once again past the Lewis's house. Two miles further on she came to a metal mailbox with the number 52 painted on it. A for-sale sign stood in the meadow behind it, showing the name of a realty company. She recognized it as a local, North Hill outfit; she'd once investigated a break-in at their office. Something else for Jeff to look into. She pulled into the sparsely graveled tracks of the drive and bumped along to the sign. When she got to it, she called Jeff and read him the agent's name and telephone number.

"Thanks," he said. "I'll try to track him down. I'm at the gas station now. The woman they thought might be our vic was a passenger in an SUV. She sat in the front while the driver pumped gas. Not exactly what you'd expect of either a vic or a perp. But they gave me the video, and I'll check it out."

To find a turnaround, she drove past the row of tall cypresses that concealed the house. Its condition startled her, despite what Middleton had said about it. A few shreds of white paint clung to the weathered boards, a number of which were hanging loose, and the tin roof had rusted a dull orange. The porch roof, also rusty, sagged in the middle atop crooked posts. A thick pelt of vines had grown up the left side of the house and spread along the front, making a shaggy garland between the two roofs.

That Alicia had even considered buying this ruin would seem to say something about the intensity of her feelings for Walter. Cynthia wondered if she'd told him her idea and he'd talked her out of it. Or maybe Middleton's objective appraisal had brought her to her senses.

She started to make the turn but changed her mind and cut the engine. She got out and climbed the porch steps. The windows that looked out onto the porch were smashed in. She peered through one with a big upright shard and saw glass bits dimly shining on the floorboards below rain-streaked, floral wallpaper. The room looked as if it had been vacant a long time. She kicked in the shard to prevent intruders from cutting themselves, and the shattering, splintering noise felt like a violation of the silence, a disturbance of the dead. She turned and headed toward the steps, but some marks on one of the inner posts caught her eye. Height marks, she realized, even before she spotted the penciled dates. They charted a child's growth from January to August in some unrecorded year. Then she noticed a lower set of marks on the opposite post. They were for the same months. Maybe the two children had lived here only for this brief memorialized period, whenever it had been. Years ago, decades.

She walked around back. The remnants of a shed and a chicken house stood in the tall meadow grass near the forest's edge. She gazed into the shadowy depths of the woods and heard in her mind the loud, seesawing rasp of cicadas. *This is why I got out of the car*, she thought. *Time to go.*

Calvary was another five miles down Mount Zion. The person who'd called in the tip, Marjorie Dobbins, lived at the north end of town in a small house almost as weathered as Alicia's house of dreams but enlivened by a red rocker on the tiny porch. Cynthia rapped on the door, and after a moment a diminutive old woman in a blue muumuu opened it. She had a sharp little beak of a nose and bright, silvery eyes.

"County sheriff's, ma'am," Cynthia said. "Are you Ms. Dobbins?"

"Yes."

"Did you call about the missing woman?"

"I did."

Cynthia took out her notebook.

A fat tabby appeared in the doorway and curled its lip at her, exposing a fang. Ms. Dobbins nudged it sideways with a slippered foot. "Now don't you go jumping on anybody's leg," she said.

Keeping an eye on the cat, Cynthia said, "You said you saw her?"

"That's right."

"When was this?"

"Sunday night."

"Where, exactly?"

"She walked right past where I was setting out there in my rocker." Ms. Dobbins glanced at her cat and said in a hushed voice, as if she didn't want it to hear, "Big Boy likes to stay out nights, but if I set in my rocker, he'll come jump on my lap, and then I got him."

"Anybody with her?"

"No. She was by herself. She never looked at me."

"And she was walking, not running?"

"Yes. But at a pretty good clip."

Cynthia glanced at the nearest streetlights. They were widely spaced, and Ms. Dobbins's house was between them. "But you could see her okay?"

"Almost as good as I see you."

"Could you describe her?"

"She was a little different from what they showed on TV, but it was her."

"How do you mean different?"

"She had blonde hair, cut like a pixie. And glasses."

That's that, Cynthia thought. She scribbled *short blonde, glasses, too dark*.

"And she had on a black jacket and blue jeans. I don't recollect her shoes."

"Okay Ms. Dobbins, thanks," Cynthia said.

"I thought she must be somebody lives in one of them trailers up the road. I don't rightly know who they belong to no more. Folks is always moving in and out. I think they all take drugs. But then I seen her on TV, and I knew it was her."

Cynthia thanked her again and got back in the car.

She still had some time on her hands, enough to make another stop. She drove past the route to the interstate and started down a little country road that led to the bottom tip of the county and Sally's farm.

Chapter 11

Meadow brook stables was a no-frills boarding farm with a hundred acres of meadow and a brook, as the name advertised. Sally had once said jokingly she should have named it Trophy Wife Stables in gratitude to her ex-husband's second wife. She'd bought the land and built the farm more than thirty years ago, using the settlement money from her divorce.

Since then she'd lived there with a succession of male companions, and based on what Bill had told her and on the two boyfriends Cynthia had known—a retired executive and a widowed ex-judge—they were all of Sally's class, or former class, but adrift in some way. They were content to live off her largesse until they weren't, or until she tired of them. The break-ups remained mysteries. The boyfriend would simply be gone one day, and no more would be said about him. Cynthia never asked for an explanation, just as Sally never inquired into the demise of Cynthia's occasional and short-lived relationships. There was a sort of pact of silence between them. Now that Sally was nearing eighty, she claimed to have put romance behind her. She had no intention, she said, of spending her last years nursing a sick old man.

They'd first met on the road Cynthia was traveling now. She was hitchhiking, and at that point no longer knew where she was, except that it was somewhere north of Alabama. She'd been sticking to back roads ever since a bad experience with a trucker. As soon as she climbed into his cab, he told her she had a pretty face and began speculating about the parts he couldn't see. She demanded to be let out, but he said to relax and enjoy the ride; they'd stop in a little while and have some fun.

He was a husky man with an outsized head and a soft, confiding voice, and when he glanced at her, his sleepy green eyes were both interested and impersonal. She'd seen an expression like that once before, and it frightened her more than his words.

She quit protesting and took stock of her situation. There was a clipboard between them on the seat with a ballpoint pen under the clip. She could use the pen as a weapon if she had to. But her best chance was to bolt as soon as he stopped the truck. She was a good runner; he wouldn't catch her. Having come up with a plan, she sat rigidly watching night fall over the highway as her captor hummed along with the radio. A half hour into the ride, she got lucky. They hit a traffic slowdown, and she grabbed her backpack and leapt from the cab, banging her knee hard against the pavement.

She still had a slight limp when Sally's red pickup pulled over for her.

"I'm Sally," Sally said, once they were underway.

"Cynthia."

"Nice to meet you, Cynthia. Hurt your leg?"

"Just tripped and hit my knee. It's okay."

"Where are you heading?"

"Canada," she said. The last book she'd read before running away from her group home was an anthology of Canadian poems. She liked the impression they gave of a place that was similar to what she knew but also different, somewhere you could forge a new identity without a lot of trouble. But the truth was she didn't know anything about Canada.

"Well, you'll hit it one of these days if you keep going in this direction. Have some family up there?"

Cynthia shook her head.

"Friends?"

"No."

"Just felt like seeing it."

"Yeah."

"My farm's a few miles up ahead, by the way. I'll have to let you out there, unless you've got time for lunch."

Cynthia, who'd been scavenging from restaurant dumpsters, accepted Sally's offer with as much restraint as she could muster. They turned at the Meadow Brook sign with its horse silhouette over a squiggle to represent the brook and went down a winding drive to a house that looked nothing like her idea of a farmhouse. The low, longish wooden structure was painted gray. It had a sort of courtyard entrance in the middle and, as it turned out, plenty of glass in the back for viewing the rolling countryside and distant mountains.

Sally led her to a tiled kitchen with a tiled table and made them sandwiches. As she was doing this, a bearded man in a bathrobe entered. He gave Cynthia a look that made her aware of how she must appear, and smell. She hadn't had a bath or changed clothes for several days now; she'd been sleeping outdoors in alleyways and under bushes.

"Claude," Sally said, "this is Cynthia. She's on her way to Canada."

"Nice country, Canada," Claude said. "My company—former company—has a branch in Toronto. Been there a number of times." He poured tomato juice into a glass and topped it with vodka.

"You want a sandwich with that?" Sally asked him.

"No, thank you, dear," Claude said.

Sally served the sandwiches and the three of them sat around the table.

"After you're done sight-seeing," Sally said to her, "then what?"

"Get a job, I guess," Cynthia answered with her mouth full.

"You want a job?"

Cynthia shrugged.

"You'll have to translate that shrug for me."

"Yes, ma'am."

"Well, we could use another stable hand, couldn't we, Claude?"

Claude, lifting his Bloody Mary to his lips, nodded.

"I don't know anything about horses or whatever," Cynthia said.

"What do you know about?"

She shrugged again.

"Not much—is that a fair translation? So it's high time you learned to do something." Sally spoke as if everything were already decided. "My stable manager, Bill, lives in a cabin behind the barn. He has an extra bedroom he might be willing to let you use, if you're quiet."

"I am quiet."

"I can see that. It's a selling point. But Bill will have to agree, of course."

He agreed to a two-week trial period, and Cynthia went to work for Sally, living in the cabin and learning her job from Bill, who also taught her to ride. When Sally discovered she was only sixteen, a fact her height had disguised, she encouraged her to get a G.E.D. and then to apply to Mary

Weaver College. She also loaned her the money for tuition and books and let her stay on at the farm, where she worked weekends and helped run the summer riding camps for kids. Bill took care of her commuting needs. He drove her the twelve miles to Calvary every weekday morning to catch the early bus to North Hill and picked her up at the bus stop in the evenings.

Cynthia parked on the circular drive in front of the house and went in through the unlocked courtyard door. She called Sally's name, which brought Maria from the kitchen. The last male resident, the judge, had been an excellent cook, and after his departure Sally had hired Maria.

"She down at the barn," Maria said, "to see how that hor is doing."

Cynthia drove herself there to save time, passing two uphill horses crisply outlined against the blue October sky. She went in through the front door and spotted Sally at one end of the darkish corridor. A tall woman, although not as tall as Cynthia, Sally had become a bit stooped in her old age. She wore her frizzy salt and pepper hair cut short in a simple style that suited her usual garb of work shoes, jeans, and a flannel shirt. She limited the wearing of dresses to special occasions, like the concerts she sometimes attended in D.C., Bill's funeral, and Cynthia's graduation from the police academy. She'd once shown Cynthia a photo album of her son, who had died of meningitis his first year in college, and there was a picture of the two of them: a smiling, chubby-faced boy in riding clothes and helmet with a show-jumping trophy in his hands; and the proud mother, her dark hair elegantly swept up and her slim figure attired in a long skirt, a short velvet jacket, and a ruffled blouse, every inch the embodiment of the horsy set.

Sally was so focused on the ailing horse, stroking his nose over the stall door, that at first she didn't notice Cynthia walking toward her. But when she did, she smiled and said, "Honey! This is a surprise. I didn't expect to see you until Sunday."

"I'm on my way to Quantico, the FBI Academy, so I thought I'd stop by. How's the horse?"

"Much better. For a while there I thought the founder had him, but he's on the mend now. Aren't you, pretty boy?"

The horse, a black stallion with a white patch on his forehead, perked his ears and fixed a beautiful dark eye on Sally.

"Your trip have anything to do with that girl who disappeared?" Sally said.

Cynthia told her the whole story down to her exile from the case.

"They'll come round one of these days, if they know what's good for them," Sally said. "Have you had lunch?"

Thinking this was how they'd met, Cynthia smiled and said, "Nope, but I've got to be going pretty soon."

"You can work in a little lunch."

Cynthia drove them back to the house, and Maria made them sandwiches and served pumpkin empanadas for dessert.

"Oh, no thanks," Cynthia said to the empanadas.

"Eat," Maria said.

"That's telling her, Maria," Sally said.

While Cynthia dutifully complied, Sally said, "I sometimes wonder what you'd have done if not for Harley."

Harley had been one of Sally's riding-camp horses, a big, brown retired hunter with a gentle disposition and a fondness for bananas. He was also the first horse Cynthia had ever ridden, and it was while taking him at a gallop through the meadow, the power of his wide body surging up her spine, that she'd felt for the first time some control over her life. He wasn't the main cause of this feeling, but he was the catalyst.

The summer after her sophomore year at Mary Weaver two boys, drunk on one father's stolen whiskey and armed with the other father's .22 rifle, had shot Harley to death. He'd come upon them in the north pasture sitting against a tree. They must have been very still for him to venture so close. One of them picked up the rifle and shot him in the head. Then they switched off until they'd put twenty bullets into his fallen body. They were arrested a few weeks later after a woman overheard them bragging to her son about the killing, which had received a lot of local attention.

By then Cynthia had submitted an application to the sheriff's department. She hadn't done it to catch the culprits, although that would have been good. She'd done it because something had clicked as she watched the responding deputies at their work. They were tactful and gentle. When Bill said of Harley, "He had hisself a good life right up till that moment," one of them—Steve Knotts, whom she knew later on—said, "I expect he did, sir. This sure is a beautiful place."

The other one, kneeling with some effort and a discreet fart to inspect Harley's wounds, first patted his great, fly-buzzed bulk. They were also efficient and methodical, asking the questions they needed to ask and searching the area for evidence. She was an English major at the college because she loved to read and because she had a glimmering that literature was a means of engaging reality, but in these deputies she witnessed another, more direct sort of engagement that she felt instinctively was right for her. Of course, the job and the people hadn't turned out to be quite what she'd imagined, but she'd never regretted her decision.

"I might've gone into teaching," she answered Sally. "Not much else you can do with an English degree. But I hope I would have ended up doing this, eventually."

"Well, then, don't let them get you down, honey. Knowing what you want—that's a great gift. Take it from me."

Chapter 12

She drove southeast through Manassas and picked up the interstate outside of Dale City. From there it was only a few miles to the Quantico exit and then a short trip through a wooded area to the guard post. A young female Marine checked her driver's license and gave her directions to the Academy, located inside the base. She drove several more miles past fields where Marines were practicing maneuvers and tan tanks were rolling. Sometimes she heard the sharp *pop-pop* of gunfire.

She stopped at a second guard post staffed by federal cops, and here she had to pull over and wait until they'd contacted the profiler. After receiving a clip-on pass, she drove to the main parking lot and walked past flags and a fountain to the central, sand-colored building. A tall man was waiting for her outside the doors.

"Detective Westbrook?" he said. "I'm Jack Slaughter, Behavioral Analysis Unit."

"Mr. Slaughter," she said neutrally, but her amusement, fueled by her irritation, must have shown in her face.

"My students think it's funny, too," he said. "At least I'm not a surgeon. Imagine hearing 'Dr. Slaughter' over the hospital intercom. Anyway, please call me Jack."

The disparity between his name and his genial manner must have figured, she thought, in his students' reaction. His appearance might have been a factor too. There was something slightly comic about it. He had sharp features, arched eyebrows and thick, silvered black hair combed straight back from a pronounced widow's peak.

He ushered her inside, and they went through more doors and down a glassed exterior walkway. "This is one of several connectors between the buildings in the main complex," he told her. "We call them the gerbil tubes."

They entered a second building and went down a hall. "Until '98," he said, "my unit was sixty feet underground, in an old nuclear bunker. The location had a certain Freudian resonance, I suppose, and a theological one too, since we deal with hell on earth here." He opened a door onto a neat though not very large office with a view of the grounds. "But I prefer my window to the symbolism."

He pointed to the guest chair and pulled his chair around the desk. "Would it be wrong to assume," he said, "that my two-cents worth means less to your boss than FBI involvement?"

"No, probably not."

His intelligent hazel eyes studied her. "And yourself?"

"This was his idea, not mine. But I appreciate your cooperation."

"And I appreciate your candor. It makes it easier to say I don't have much." He picked up a hand-written sheet on his desk, glanced at it, and put it back. "No bodies. Nothing caught on camera. No witnesses— except for the one who saw a car that may or may not have been used in the abduction. On the other hand, the absence of information tells us something. It indicates an organized, careful perpetrator, or perpetrators. He, or they—I lean toward a single person, so let's say *he*—may have stalked his victims for some time, possibly weeks or months, to determine the safest public place to take them. A public place is never really safe, of course; other people can show up and spoil things. He may have had to put off abducting them more than once, which would indicate considerable control over his impulses, not good for us. Also, if he knew the victims' routines that well, he likely could have attacked them in a house or an office, so that would suggest he's either a necrophile like Bundy or a sadist who enjoys taking his time. For their sakes I hope he's the former."

"Why do you think it's one perpetrator?"

"Because it usually is. Serial killers, the ones motivated by sex, are enacting their private sexual fantasies. Also, the victims in this case seem to fit a very particular fantasy. They were all in their early to mid-thirties. The last one was the youngest at thirty-two. They were attractive, but not in their absolute prime, biologically speaking. A killer after a sort of generic desirability might be drawn to younger women."

"What's the fantasy?"

"I don't know, but I'd say it has to do with his mother. Many sons hit puberty when their mothers are around that age."

"So he hates his mother."

"Yes, but his feelings could be more complex than that. He could be attracted to her, too, assuming I'm right about the significance of her age, which I may not be."

She pulled out her notebook and jotted all this down.

"I'd speculate too that his mother is a businesswoman or a professional of some kind. The victims were a self-employed CPA, the owner of a travel agency, and a college teacher. Since he appears to take his time stalking his victims, he might also put some time into choosing them. And he could be a professional himself, out of a desire to please his mother. Or the opposite could be true. He could be dependent on her in order to persuade himself that she loves him."

Thinking of Freddy, she said, "How old would you say he is?"

"Old enough to have honed his skills—I'd guess at least his late twenties, and probably older. Usually there's an escalation to the enactment of the deepest fantasies. Self-exposure or voyeurism first, followed by more serious stuff, maybe an unsuccessful attempt at rape or kidnapping, or a murder that was amateurish by the killer's present standards, that he was lucky to get away with. Any unsolved cases along those lines in the last few years?"

"No attempted kidnappings. As far as I can remember, the only murdered women besides these three, in the last ten years, anyway, were the victims of domestic violence. But I'll check. And I'll have a look at the rapes again."

"There might also be a juvenile record. Stealing, arson, cruelty to animals or other children."

She wrote this down too. "Anything else?"

"His M.O. not only allows him to keep his victims for a longer time—and I'm assuming he takes them to some private place of his own—but it creates quite a stir in the media: people disappearing in public. It's part of the thrill for him. I'm sure he's following your investigation very closely. It wouldn't hurt to flatter him a little in your public statements. Refer to him as highly intelligent, et cetera. And one other thing. The signs of struggle at the scenes indicate that he subdued these women physically. He could be large or quite strong, or both."

Now she thought of Walter Lewis breathless on the telephone. "The report I sent you on the last case," she said, "doesn't go into possible suspects, but one of them is a man in his mid-thirties, fit looking, who exercises. He and the victim were friends and may have been lovers, and he doesn't have a firm alibi for the night of her disappearance. But he does for the first two abductions; he was living on the west coast at the time."

Slaughter raised an arched eyebrow. "How possible a suspect is he?"

She told him about Walter Lewis.

"A poet?" he said.

"That was my partner's reaction too."

"Still, something about the third case does seem a little off to me."

"How so?"

"The timing, for one thing. The first victim disappeared on a Saturday, the second on a Friday, and this one on a Sunday. There's a grouping around the weekend, which could mean the killer works during the week. If he does, he would have had a day or more with the first two."

"But only a few hours with Alicia Bradford."

"Yes. Also, she's more or less the right age, but in her pictures, at least, she looks younger. There's an innocence about her. And although she's a professional like the other two women, her job is sort of rarified compared to theirs. Academia can be cutthroat, I know from experience—I taught at UVA for a few years before coming here. But it isn't the same as dealing with ordinary business realities. She might have lacked a suitable aura, if you will—the extra quality that would appeal to him. Actually, you're more his type."

"Pardon me?"

"Your job anchors you in the real world more than just about anybody's. And if you don't mind my saying so, you have the right physical characteristics."

"Like being past my prime?"

His eyes widened in alarm. "I'm sorry. I didn't mean—"

"I know. I'm joking."

"Oh."

"Other thoughts?"

"Well, just that you should take my comments with several grains of salt. Serial killers aren't necessarily consistent. They may change their M.O.'s or their victim types. They may even stop killing, for a while or forever."

"Okay. Thanks." She put her notebook away.

"Would you like something to drink?"

"No, that's—"

"The vending machines are just down the hall."

What's the hurry, she thought. Unless Jeff had learned something, all that awaited her was writing up another report.

"One of them a coffee machine?" she said.

"Yes, but the coffee's awful."

"Good. That's what I'm used to."

Before she could say anything else, he was out the door. She looked around his office. No diplomas or citations on the walls. A sickly potted plant on the windowsill. A six-inch Freddy Krueger—Freddy—standing atop the filing cabinet. A small picture frame on the desk. She turned it around and saw a photo of a teenaged girl sitting in a boat. She had Slaughter's sharp features, but in her case the effect was pretty rather than comic.

"That's my daughter Anna," he said behind her. "She's going off to college next year, and I'll see even less of her than I do now. She lives with her mother."

He handed her a paper cup of coffee. "I forgot to ask about cream and sugar, but I think there're some packets in my desk."

"I'm good," she said.

He sat down holding an unopened can of Coke.

"You going to drink that?" she said.

"Not until you taste your coffee. You might want a substitute."

She sipped the terrible coffee. "It's fine."

"Sure?"

"Yep."

He opened the Coke. "How long have you been with the sheriff's department?"

"Fourteen years. Eight in uniform, five in Property Crimes, and now Crimes Against Persons."

"Still like what you do?"

She nodded. "I'd like it better if we could solve these disappearances. What about you? Still like your job?"

"Not so much."

"No?"

"I got into it because I was fascinated with abnormal psychology and evil—still a necessary word, it seems to me. But after years of looking at crime-scene photos and interviewing killers and seeing the videos some of them made of their victims, not to mention thinking about terrorists, which is what I do most of the time now—" He smiled ruefully. "—evil has lost its charm, I'm afraid. And I'm not even on the front lines like you. How do you do it, day after day?"

"I don't. I do it day by day. Some days are better than others."

"You never feel like getting out?"

"No. Not yet, anyway." She glanced at her watch. "Well, I won't keep you any longer."

He walked her back out to the lobby of the main building. Holding the door open, he said, "Anything you want to run by me, I'd be happy to look at."

"Thank you."

"Sorry about unloading on you."

She waved her hand dismissively. "It's a tough job."

He started to say something and stopped himself. Then he said, "Good luck."

"Thanks."

As she went down the steps, she heard the close, echoing sound of gunfire.

Chapter 13

*S*he's the one. He knew it the instant he saw her. He likes it that she's tall, and now that he thinks of it, he was vaguely aware of a tall woman in the other televised press conferences. But there were no close-ups of her. He couldn't see her high cheekbones and big, serious brown eyes, or her long ponytail. Most of all, he couldn't see her confidence. It shows in the way she looks at you with those serious eyes, in the way she moves. She doesn't swagger, but she comes close. And there's something else. He felt it because it's true of him too. She's all about control. It's what defines her. She won't break easily, he's certain, and that's why he must have her.

But he isn't sure how to go about it. The fact that she's a detective complicates things. She carries a gun and knows how to use it. She also has a kind of alertness the other women lacked. If he follows her around, she might catch him at it. And even if his stalking skills prevail over her detective's instincts, her working hours, which he supposes are variable and irregular, will make it hard to trail her when he's free. But these difficulties only fuel his desire.

He consults the local phone books at the library—no computer trail for him—and finds her right away in the Parkerville directory. An apartment address. He commits it to memory, though he isn't sure how he'll use it. That night lying in bed, he tries to think of a plan. Nothing comes to him, but a few hours later he wakes up with the beginning of one. It's a little flame that must be fed. He dresses, goes out to his car, and drives through the darkness, feeling as he does at such times a calm expansiveness. No danger yet, just the freedom of going about his true work. That work has given him a detailed knowledge of Parkerville, and he finds her apartment without any trouble. It's in a complex of three brick-and-wood buildings facing inward toward a parking strip and a small central plot of grass. There are stairwells for every four apartments, two down and two up, in the usual arrangement. Her number designates a bottom apartment. He drives slowly past it. A blue compact, license number *SY4*-something, occupies her parking slot. The adjacent visitor space is empty, but whether this means she lives alone he can't be sure. He feels she lives alone. It's another thing, he realizes now, that drew him to her—the solitude that enfolds her, the sense that she doesn't need anyone. He glances at her dark window and imagines her sleeping inside, her dreams untroubled by any thoughts of him.

He leaves the complex and parks on the street near the exit. It's five a.m., but his brain is whirring. He mulls over the idea that brought him here: mastering her in her apartment. If he can manage it, he'll have less time with her than he'd like, and more important, he'll need to keep the gag on. But he knows her; he'll be able to read her journey in her eyes. And maybe at the end, when all he can read in them is despair, he'll rip the tape from her lips and, with his hands around her throat, let her speak.

At 7:15 the blue compact *SY4* turns onto the street in the direction of the sheriff's office. He starts his engine and drives the other way to a convenience store. Using the phone outside it, he calls her home number. No answer. He drives around for a few minutes and calls again from a gas station, with the same result. No one lives with her, as he suspected. He returns to the complex, parks near the dumpsters at the front, and walks behind her building. A high privacy fence runs the length of it. He goes to the fence and pretends to inspect it. When he walks back, he looks at the building. The first-story apartments have patios separated by wooden walls and sheltered to a degree by the second-floor balconies. The patio door he can see, which must be standard for the complex, isn't a sliding door; it's an ordinary door with a glass-paneled top half. He feels a surge of excitement. Once he's on her patio, the walls and the overhanging balcony and the fence will shield him from view, and although he's never broken into a place, he's positive he can get into this one.

Driving home, he fills in the details of his plan. It's one he could implement today, if he knew more about her habits. But deep down he feels that he knows enough already. And since he's moved this far outside his comfort zone—forsaken his M.O., as the police call it, for something more risky and improvisational—why not go for the prize? Unless something comes up, she will have put in a full day by five, and he doesn't think she'll be bringing anybody home. She's not the type. She may fuck men, but she won't let them into her inner sanctum. Anyway, he can watch for her through a front window and leave if necessary by the patio door. But it won't be necessary. She'll swagger in, and he'll have her. And coming on the heels of the last press conference, her story will dominate the media. He could write the lead himself: Detective investigating serial murders found murdered.

He's curious, too, about what they'll make of his new M.O. Will they speculate that there's another killer in the county? If they do, they'll be getting it right for the wrong reason, and this will be his little joke on them.

The first thing he does when he gets home is eat breakfast. He's famished. He has hot chocolate, cereal with banana, and a couple of energy bars. Then he does a light workout to relax, makes a call, showers and shaves, and leaves again around ten. He needs to buy a few items, and he doesn't want to get them all in one town. An excess of caution, maybe, but he's venturing into new territory. Also, he has a few hours to kill before going back to her apartment. He wants to be there with enough time to set up his little surprise, but not so much that he grows careless.

He drives to stores in three different towns. The last cashier to serve him is extremely slow. She's a fat young woman with a streak of purple in her black hair and long curling purple fingernails that make it difficult for her to press the register keys. But he doesn't complain or show his impatience in any way. It's best to remain unmemorable. He amuses himself by imagining how she'd react if he leaned in and whispered why he was buying a toolbox. Would she giggle nervously, thinking it was a very strange joke? Or would she see the truth in his eyes and stand there dumbstruck and terrified, her fingernails curled at her sides like flimsy, useless claws?

Too bad he'll never know. He'll have to content himself with the inevitable TV interviews of the shocked but tedious neighbors.

He puts the toolbox in his trunk, opens it up, and transfers to it the rubber mallet he purchased earlier. He lifts the cover on the spare tire and moves the stuff he keeps there into the box too: a small knife, duct tape, two pairs of handcuffs, and a stun gun. At home again, he puts one or two other things in the box. For the most part he'll use her things. This will reduce the chances of leaving something of his behind.

He takes his new clothes out of the shopping bag, cuts off the tags, and dresses in front of the exercise-room mirror. What he sees confirms his theory: the simplest disguise is best. A stranger in blue work clothes and a blue cap stares back at him—a man who looks somehow younger than himself, who appears at ease in his body, full of confidence. A lady killer, perhaps. The young handyman smiles at the joke.

He looks outside, sees no one, and hurries to his car carrying the toolbox. It's a glorious day. As he drives, yellow leaves flitter over the road like butterflies. The sky is a deep, intense blue. He glimpses the potent silhouette of a hawk high in a tree. It's as if he's shucked off an outer shell that filtered the light.

When he arrives at her complex, he cruises past the dumpsters and parks near the end of the building closer to her apartment. Sitting in his car, he looks around. An old woman across the way hobbles toward a stairwell. After she disappears from view, he grabs the toolbox and climbs out. There's a space between Cynthia Westbrook's building and the one at right angles to it. His heart pounding, he walks toward the gap in no particular haste, like a handyman on a mundane service call, come to fix a patio wall or a broken door-pane.

Chapter 14

She drove straight to headquarters intending to write her report and be done with it. Jeff wasn't back yet, which could mean that one aspect of her plan had worked; he was doing something with the pretty teller. But if he was, it might be better to interrupt him now rather than later. She rang his number.

A woman answered, not a young woman.

"Hi," Cynthia said. "Is Jeff there?"

"Yes, but he—"

"Gimme the phone, Momma," Jeff said in the background. "Cyn?"

"Yeah."

"Hey, I was going to call you in a while. I had a little accident. Well, not so little. Broke my leg in a few places."

"Jesus. What happened?"

"I was driving back to North Hill from the county hospital—another story—when this car coming toward me runs off the road and hits a tree. I brake and pull over, and I see a skinny white guy staggering up the embankment into the woods. Then a cop car shows up and the cops jump out with their guns drawn. Man, it was like old times. I jump out too and run across the road. I flash my badge, tell 'em what I saw, and we fan out through the woods. I spot the guy maybe twenty yards ahead, still kind of listing. I'm going down a slope, and as I reach for my gun my foot snags on a root and I spin forward and hear this loud crack. Knew I was in trouble before I hit the ground."

"Where are you now?"

"The hospital again. Surgery in the morning."

"Surgery?"

"Yeah. But you haven't heard the worst part. Some other cops showed up, and one of them was Eeps."

"Oops."

"Uh-huh. The first cops caught the guy—he'd hijacked the car from a pregnant woman, yanked her out by the hair. And while they were taking him in, Eeps and his partner waited with me for the ambulance. Eeps was loving it, talking about his sore ankle from the other morning and asking if we'd found any important cigarette butts. Then the other cop, not that Williams who eyeballed you but a doofus whose cousin played second-string on my high-school football team—he recognized me, and they started talking about how blacks got all the glory in school sports and it was discrimination against the white boys. I wanted to say it was our superior genes, on account of our ancestors surviving the slave ships and all. That would have got 'em going. But at the moment I didn't exactly look like an example of superior genes. So I said it was a shame that two half-wits didn't equal a whole wit."

"And they didn't shoot you?"

"I waited until the ambulance crew got there to say it."

"Wise decision. Want me to come stand guard?"

"If Eeps and the doofus show, you could guard them from my mother."

"Okay. See you in a few minutes."

*****

Jeff and his mother were reading sections of the newspaper when she arrived. Jeff's right leg was sheathed in a blue cast and propped on a pillow. Mrs. White, a stout little woman, stood and gave her a big smile.

"Jeff didn't tell me you were so tall," she said.

"Thanks, Momma."

"What did I say?"

"Nice to meet you," Cynthia said. And to Jeff, "They give you some idea of the recovery time?"

"Yeah. Assuming I survive the surgery—"

"Oh, hush now," Mrs. White said.

"Wheelchair for a couple of weeks, then a walker and crutches for another eight weeks. And therapy after that."

"He'll be staying with me," Mrs. White said. "So at least I can get some good food in him."

"She aims to cure my fried-chicken deficiency," Jeff said.

"What were you doing at the hospital before the accident?" Cynthia said.

Mrs. White started toward the door.

"You don't have to go," Cynthia said.

"I'd rather not know y'alls business, thank you. There's a sitting room at the end of the hall. I'll be there."

Jeff waited until his mother had left. "First thing I did after you gave me the realtor's number," he said, "was look at the gas station tape. The guy who runs the station is Asian, and all white women must look alike to him. Only way the woman in the tape could be our vic was if she'd aged thirty years between seven and nine p.m. So I chalked that off the list and called the realtor. He said he'd had one conversation with Alicia on the phone. He assumed she was just interested in the lot since according to him the house is a wreck."

"It is."

"By then, it was past noon. I dropped in on Denise, Ms. Johnson, at the bank, and she agreed to have lunch with me during her break at one."

"Ah ha."

He grinned. "After lunch, I went by Freddy's. One of the boarders told me he was in the county hospital. Heart attack. So I drove there—I mean, here. He's on the floor beneath us, if you want to say hi."

"You talk to him?"

"For about ten seconds. I asked him why he was at the press conference, and he started telling me that Sampson looked like this actor who'd played a cop, and then he dozed off. I headed back to North Hill to find some of Walt's students. And that's when I screwed myself. But the day wasn't a total loss, maybe. Denise told me some interesting stuff."

"Oh?"

"She said a Detective Smith had been in to see the loan guy."

"Smith? Who's he?"

"Right. I don't know any Smith, either, although you think there'd be at least one Smith in the division. So I asked her to describe him. Big man, brown suit, bags under his eyes."

"Fallon."

"Had to be. At the press conference you told him and the Bradfords about the loan appointment, and Alicia could have mentioned her bank to him, but I bet he was tailing us yesterday. Once or twice I had a feeling, you know? He might have seen us stop at the branch before he went on to the press conference. And that's not all. Denise asked me if the loan guy, Middleton, was a suspect. I said no, but did she have some reason to think he should be? She said not really, but she'd caught him staring through his blinds at some of the women customers with a kind of creepy expression."

"She tell you anything else about him?"

"He's super polite, she says. He never talks about himself—sort of like you in that respect. And he started there in September."

"Four months before the first abduction. That's roughly consistent with the time between the later abductions. Where'd he come from, did she know?"

"A Southland branch in Maryland." Jeff reached over to the bed table and picked up his notepad. "Frederick. That's just over the state line, isn't it?"

"Yeah. Did she happen to hear what Fallon asked Middleton?"

"Middleton wasn't there. He'd called in sick."

"Hmm. Okay. Maybe he's worth a look. I'll do it in the morning if I get a chance." She laid her hand lightly on his cast. "How many breaks is a few?"

"Four. Big one in the femur, smaller ones around the ankle."

She grimaced in sympathy.

"How'd your day go, by the way?" he said.

"Better than yours. But my tip was bad, too."

"And the profiler—he didn't crack the case?"

She shook her head, unwilling to pile on Jack Slaughter now that she'd met him. He'd treated her visit seriously even though he'd guessed the reason behind it.

"I'll see you tomorrow," she said.

She went down the hall and said goodbye to Mrs. White.

"He'd never tell you," Mrs. White said, "but he thinks a whole lot of you."

"And vice-versa. We make a good team."

"But he never said you were so tall."

*****

Driving home she thought about Jeff's comparison of her to Middleton. True, she didn't talk much about herself, but Sally had never pressed her to do it, and despite his teasing neither had Jeff. She felt they accepted her on her own terms. Other people, however, might regard her as aloof. She wondered if that was how Jack Slaughter saw her.

When she switched on the light in her apartment she saw the place from a stranger's point of view: the plainness, the absence of anything that would be identified as personal except the two small photos on the lamp table. That is, unless you counted the books. A stranger could safely conclude that the occupant liked to read. Cheap metal bookcases lined the living-room walls, their shelves filled and double filled and their tops bearing stacks of books. Her apartment, it occurred to her, was an even more Spartan version of Alicia's.

She left her jacket and holster on the couch and poured herself a glass of red wine in the kitchen. As she was doing this, one of the private jets that used the county airport passed over, much lower than usual by the sound of it. She paused until the drone had peaked, then finished filling her glass and carried it to the couch. *Poor Jeff*, she thought. *He was funny and stoic about his leg, but being out of action for so long would be hard on him.*

She kicked off her shoes and, sipping the wine, went over her impressions of Middleton. Distracted by his information about the house, she hadn't paid much attention to him. He was around her age, medium height, medium build, light-brown hair and light-colored eyes, gray or green. The eyes were a little wide set and the chin somewhat pointed, giving him a faintly elfin appearance. But he was neither handsome nor homely. Unremarkable. His polite, professional manner had been unremarkable too. Also, his surprise at Alicia's disappearance had seemed genuine. But of course if he were the killer, he'd want to give that impression. She remembered his firm handshake. Quite a strong grip, actually. Jack Slaughter had said the killer might be large or strong.

Her glass was nearly empty, although she could only remember taking the first sip. She set it on the coffee table, put her feet up, and closed her eyes. Her thoughts shifted to Jack Slaughter. He was a sensitive man. A lonely one too. He'd made a point of letting her know he was divorced. Behind her eyelids she could feel the world receding, leaving her alone with herself.

She was standing in the backyard of the forsaken house, and from everywhere in the dusk came the pulsing chorus of the cicadas. The sound grew louder and louder until the walls of her chest were vibrating with it.

She started awake and kicked the glass off the coffee table. Her first conscious thought was that the jet had been too loud. She slipped her gun from the holster and went into the kitchen. The window over the sink was closed and locked. She pulled up the blinds that covered the back door's mullioned top half. Every pane held a dark image of the room except the one nearest the doorknob. She probed it with her gun, and the barrel slipped through like Alice through the looking glass. She tried the knob. Unlocked.

She snapped off the safety on her gun, switched on the outside light, and pulled the door open. The patio was empty. She stepped to the edge and looked both ways down the grassy corridor. All she saw were rectangles of light spilling from other doors and windows. Turning around, she noticed a flat gray object and probed it with her foot. It was a patch of duct tape with fragments of the missing pane stuck to it.

Her gun at her side, finger off the trigger, she went back in and checked the pantry and the small front closet and the bathroom. She took a deep breath and entered the bedroom. Some things lay on the carpet near the bed. She guessed their purpose, but couldn't focus on them now. She slid open the closet doors and looked under the clothes. She dropped to the carpet and checked under the bed. Tied high on each leg was a short piece of white nylon cord ending in an open slip noose.

She stood and went around the bed and examined the things on the floor. They were lined up like surgical instruments: carving knife, scissors, pliers, screwdriver, bottle of rubbing alcohol, matches, can of Sterno, and a hairbrush she recognized as her own. Then she realized they all belonged to her. She was staring at a torture kit—excepting the hairbrush, for which she couldn't readily assign a purpose—assembled from the things in her apartment.

Chapter 15

She could feel her heart throbbing in her throat as she moved from the bedroom to the front door and pressed her back against it. From there she could see all the way to the patio door. Keeping her eye on it, she tried to think. Her first thought was a question: Why had he left? He, a lone intruder, being what she imagined. Maybe he'd only wanted to frighten her, but his preparations seemed too thorough for that, the break-in too risky. Which suggested either a change of heart, impossible to believe, or a forced exit of some kind. But what kind? Her mind skipped to another question: Why her? There had to be a connection to the kidnappings. The planned sadistic murder of a female cop investigating the disappearances of three women—it was too big a coincidence.

But did this mean her perp was the women's killer? He had a different M.O., in the ways she could compare. An attack in a private rather than a public place, seemingly with the intention of committing the murder there. And if he was the same person, he'd shortened the time between attacks from several months to two days. But Jack Slaughter had said that M.O.'s weren't set in stone. He'd also said she was more the killer's type than Alicia Bradford. Maybe the killer had been disappointed in Alicia— too youthful looking, too innocent—and decided to strike again when he saw her. In which case he would have to be someone who'd noticed her during this investigation; otherwise, he would have come after her before now. Not that this narrowed the field of suspects very much. He could be anyone she'd interviewed in the last two days, anyone at the press conference and, depending on whether the TV coverage had shown her, anyone in the area with a TV. Any male, she corrected herself. But she couldn't think about the men she wasn't aware of. Sticking to the ones she knew, she put together a short list: Freddy, a few college kids at his place, Walter, Gilley, and Middleton.

Gilley struck her as too peripheral and the students as too young. Freddy was less peripheral. Also, depending on when he'd been admitted to the hospital, his heart attack might explain her intruder's exit; he could have become ill while laying out the torture kit. She got her jacket and the phone book and resumed her place by the door. She took the cell from her jacket pocket, looked up the hospital number and called it. Admissions told her an ambulance had brought Freddy in around ten p.m. yesterday. Not Freddy, then.

She was down to Walter and Middleton, hypothetically. But Walter hadn't moved here until June. If he'd killed Alicia, he must have done it for reasons involving their relationship, and the similarity of his crime to the other two was either an accident or an attempt to mislead the police. What, then, would be his motive for torturing and killing a cop? She'd made him angry, but the preparations of her intruder went way beyond anger. Nevertheless, she got out her notebook and found his number. This time he answered.

"Mr. Lewis," she said, "Investigator Westbrook. I'd like you to come in for another interview. I have some more questions for you."

There was a sound like a door shutting. "Questions about what?"

"Your relationship with Alicia Bradford, what you did in North Hill that night."

When he didn't respond, she said, "Don't you want to clear the air, Mr. Lewis?"

More silence.

"I'll take that as a no," she said.

"What happens if I don't come in?" he said.

"I think you should."

"I'm going to hang up now."

And he did.

She'd heard nothing in his voice except resentment and distrust. No tincture of any other feeling toward her, and no hint that he was concealing knowledge of the break-in. If he'd done it, he was a great actor, which of course he might be.

She looked up Middleton's phone number and address, wrote them down in her notebook, and called him. After a few rings, a recorded voice, not his, gave his number and asked the caller to leave a message at the tone. She hung up.

What now? Her thoughts circled back to the cause of her perp's departure. Maybe someone had scared him off, but it wouldn't be someone merely knocking on the door. She called the manager.

"Mr. Luce," she said, "this is Cynthia Westbrook in 26 A. Did you have to go in my apartment today for any reason?"

"No, ma'am. Is there a problem?"

"Somebody broke in. I thought maybe you'd chased them away without realizing it."

"A break-in? You call the police?"

"I am the police."

"Oh, I forgot."

"You notice any strangers around today?"

"No ma'am. But I was mainly in the office."

"Thanks."

When she hung up, Mike Fallon popped into her head. He'd tried to talk to Middleton at the bank. Maybe he'd been looking into him and would know something. She called Fallon's motel and asked to be put through to his room. No answer.

She slipped on her gun holster and jacket and shoes and went out and began knocking on doors. Her neighbors had either been absent during the day or hadn't seen anything. The last door she tried was Mrs. Morelli's.

"What do you want?" Mrs. Morelli said, her watery eye staring accusingly over the chain.

"Hi, I'm Cynthia, from across the way. I was wondering—"

"You interrupted my dinner."

"Sorry. I just need to know whether you—"

"It's hard for me to get up."

"I apologize. Did you see any strangers around here today, or anyone acting suspiciously?"

"No, I didn't see nothing. How many times do I have to say it?"

"Once is plenty. Thanks."

Facing the shut door, she considered her next move. She got in her car and called headquarters. Rick Draper answered. She told him about the break-in and asked for a tech to process her apartment for prints, in particular the back door, the broken pane, and certain objects on the bedroom floor, which she described.

"What is this," Rick said, "some kinda sick joke?"

"I don't think so."

"Then why didn't they—"

"Good question. I'm looking into it, so I won't be there. But the tech can get in through the patio door. And I want an APB on Michael Fallon, Maryland plates."

"The vic's uncle? You think he did it?"

"No, but he might have some information. Call me if you tag him."

She drove to the Wayside Inn outside of North Hill. The motel, a single-story horseshoe structure, had seen better days and probably less scruffy clerks than the wizened, pony-tailed man who gave her Fallon's room number. She walked down to the room. The parking space in front of it was empty and the curtained window was dark, but she knocked anyway and called Fallon's name. She waited and knocked again. Then she went back to the car and got her kit bag from the trunk. She put it on the seat beside her, pulled out a phone book and the GPS, looked up Middleton's address, and entered it in the GPS. The map showed it on the other end of town, only a mile or two north of Alicia's place.

Middleton's second-story apartment was in a complex that had also seen better days—not what she would have imagined for a banker. And like Fallon, he appeared to be gone. No car in the parking spot, no light in the window. But she climbed the stairwell, thinking that this wasn't the ideal place to take a victim, who would have to be ambulatory, compliant, and not noticeably restrained. She knocked, waited, and went back down to her car.

She phoned the hospital to see if Middleton, who'd called in sick today, might be there. He wasn't. While she had them on the line, she made the same query about Fallon, in case he'd been in a drunk-driving accident. He wasn't there, either. She called headquarters again. Jimmy Smoot told her that Rick had gone with the tech to her apartment and no one had spotted Fallon yet. She asked him to find the number of the Frederick, Maryland, CID, and he got it for her.

She rang the number and identified herself.

"No, kidding," said the kidder on the other end. "What a coincidence. I'm an investigator myself."

"Does the name David G. Middleton mean anything to you?" she said.

"Nope."

"He used to work at a Southland bank there. I don't know for how long, but he left about a year ago."

"Lemme check last year's phone book. Okay, I got a David G. Middleton at 1460 Willow."

She wrote this down. "He have a record?"

"Just a sec. Uh-uh. Not even a parking ticket. He's as clean as anybody who's never been caught."

While she'd been waiting for his answer, two facts had coalesced in her mind: the relative closeness of Frederick to North Hill, and the unsuitability of Middleton's apartment for a kidnapper's purposes. "Can you find out who owns that house now?" she said.

"I can Google the White Pages. No, nothing there. But it could just mean there's no landline. Property assessments might show something. Yeah, here it is. No names given, but the house last changed ownership in December 2008."

"So if Middleton was living in it last year, it must still belong to him."

"He's in Virginia now?"

"Right."

"Probably renting it out, then."

She didn't suggest the possibility that had inspired her question, partly because something else had occurred to her: Why buy a house and move away after less than a year? Maybe the job in North Hill paid more, but she doubted it. North Hill was smaller than Frederick. She remembered Jack Slaughter's comment about the learning curve of a serial killer.

"You got any unsolved rapes or murders of women," she asked, "over, say, the last two years?"

"Oh, sure. Half a dozen rapes, one murder."

"Were any of the victims white brunettes in their thirties?"

"The murder vic was. I know because I worked the case. Bastard cut her throat in a parking lot, nearly took off her head. We treated it as a robbery homicide since her purse was missing."

"When was this?"

"January of last year."

Middleton had moved to North Hill in September of last year. Was it because he'd botched a kidnapping attempt and been afraid to try again in Fredrick? And now she wondered something else: The parking-lot murder had occurred a month after he bought the house. Had he bought it as a place to take victims?

She said, "Can you find out if he has an earlier Frederick address?"

"There's a search engine might do the trick. You got a date of birth?"

"No, but I'd guess between '70 and '80."

The detective hummed a tune that sounded vaguely like "Strangers in the Night." "Here we go," he said. "David G. Middleton, born May 12, '74. He has two other local addresses—doesn't mean they're all still his. One's an apartment, and the other's in a… hey, that's interesting."

"What?"

"I was about to say the other's in a pricey neighborhood, and then I remembered we arrested a woman named Middleton who lived there. Must've been fifteen, sixteen years ago. She owned a nursing home, and we got a report that one of their stiffs was in a bad way, in addition to being dead. Funeral home said the guy's skin came off with his socks, they'd been on him so long. So we paid the place a visit, and it was a real horror show. Patients tied up, filth and starvation. To save his ass the assistant director cut a deal with the D.A., and that opened up a whole other can of worms. Medicare fraud, unauthorized use of patients' funds, every possible way of squeezing money out of the joint. Cherie— that was the woman's name, Cherie Middleton. She was quite a fox too. I remember the paper had a line about her—'lovely but lethal.' Like she was a movie star instead of a cold-hearted bitch."

"Where is she now?"

"That I couldn't tell you. She croaked before the trial, of natural causes. Don't remember what, but it was something fast, like a stroke."

"Okay, thanks. You've been a big help."

"No problemo. You know, you sound pretty hot for a cop. Ever feel the urge for a little phone sex, gimme a call. Ask for Detective Decker."

"Don't hold your breath, Detective Decker."

She hung up and sat in the car trying to figure out what she had. Nothing, really, except speculation. But instead of dismissing it, she found herself adding to it. Suppose Fallon, out looking for Middleton, had ended up tailing him to her apartment, taken him prisoner, and learned about the Frederick house from him. That would explain both her intruder's absence and neither man being home. She plugged Middleton's current Frederick address into the GPS. It was forty-one miles away. She could get there by nine, and if it turned out to be a wild goose chase, as it probably would, no one would be the wiser. It would remain her private folly.

The flat female voice of the GPS guided her back to Parkerville and north toward Maryland on US-15. As she drove, she tried to fit her thoughts about Middleton into a coherent narrative. In accordance with Jack Slaughter's theorizing, Cherie Middleton had been an attractive professional like the three victims, and Middleton had chosen an occupation his avaricious mother might have respected. Following her death, he'd become more and more obsessed with homicidal fantasies and finally bought a house in which to realize them, but his first victim had proved uncooperative and he'd panicked and murdered her on the spot.

After that, he'd moved to North Hill for safety's sake, but he'd hung onto the Frederick house because it was useful. He could kidnap his victims in Virginia and torture and kill them in Maryland, without showing his face there very much. Drive in and drive out. Easy if he had an attached garage. This could account, too, for his run-down apartment building. The necessity of paying both mortgage and rent might have dictated his living arrangements in North Hill.

Her belief in this scenario, and in Fallon's kidnapping of Middleton, flared momentarily like the road signs in her headlights. The rest of the time she felt she was chasing chimeras through the dark. Outside of Frederick the GPS started talking again, telling her to continue on the re-named route, to keep right, to turn left, and to turn left again in point-seven miles at her destination. Disobeying the last instruction, she stopped a block short of the address, tested the small flashlight she carried in her jacket, and walked to the house.

It was a clapboard rancher with a projecting attached garage on the left. Above it, a pale patch of luminescence marked the moon's position. The front windows were dark. She cut across the adjacent yard and went around back, where she spotted a window flushed with faint light. The discovery made the hairs on her neck prickle; her imagination seemed to be turning real. But she reminded herself that Middleton could have rented the place, as Decker had suggested.

She moved along the house to the window and peered through the slit between the curtains. Mike Fallon was sitting at one end of a table, his somber profile and white shirt dimly aglow. The source of the light was an open doorway opposite him. His sleeves were rolled up, and his bare forearms rested on the table. His big hands flanked a liquor bottle. She could see a side holster with a gun in it. She knew he was really there, but she couldn't quite believe it, and his utter stillness added to his apparitional quality. She felt as if she might blink him away.

She went to the end of the house and called 911. A dog began to bark while she whispered her request, but it was far enough away that she didn't have to raise her voice. Then she returned to the window. Fallon was still there, motionless as a wax figure. She'd watch him until the cops arrived. But the moment she thought this, he rose unsteadily and headed toward the doorway. Entering its frame, he seemed to shrink. He was going down some stairs, she realized. She needed to act now.

She hurried past the window, found a door, and tried it. Locked. She squared her shoulders and kicked it hard with the flat of her foot. It gave a little, absorbing the shock. She kicked it again and this time it flew inward upon darkness. She pulled out her flashlight and her gun and stepped into a kitchen.

The door on the left had a pale strip of light under it. She stood to one side of it, yanked it open, and peered around the frame at the table and the lighted doorway. She glided by the table, everything in slow motion now, her eyes scooping up the empty bottle's amber sheen, a red smear on the table top, more smears on the bare floor, a black radio with twin speakers on a chair. She floated down the stairs into a familiar rank effluvium of blood and shit.

Chapter 16

Her apartment is small and full of books, not what he expected somehow, though on second thought the books make sense: she prefers them to people. Still wearing the latex gloves he slipped on before the break-in, he does a walk-through of the kitchen, living room, and bathroom. He wants to get the lay of the land, but he also wants to touch her things—which are now his for the duration. He hasn't had this experience, not at this level of possession. He handles an empty glass vase, a dog-eared paperback titled mrs. Dalloway lying on the coffee table, a cardboard checker box on the shelf under it, a framed snapshot of an old white woman and a tiny old black man, and another of a horse in a field. In the bathroom he opens the cabinet over the sink and finds, along with the usual medicines, a few cosmetics. He rubs a cool tube of lipstick over his lips and washes it off.

He returns to the kitchen and searches the drawers for items he can use, sticking them in the toolbox. When he's done, he carries the box into her bedroom. He's saved the bedroom for last, but like the rest of the apartment, it's something of a disappointment. Minimal furnishings, beige curtains, a white bedspread. The only wall decoration is her police academy diploma. He didn't know what he'd discover, but it wasn't this. He puts the toolbox down and opens the folding closet doors. He runs a gloved hand across her clothes, stops at a silky black dress, and gathers it to his nose. Breathing in her scent, he imagines ripping the dress off of her. Maybe he can manage that.

He lets go of the fabric and walks over to the dresser. There's a hairbrush on top, wooden with black bristles. He picks it up. It's lighter than the one his mother hit him with the time he tried to tell her about his perfect math score. He remembers the pain, as much as anyone can remember pain, but it was nothing compared to her calling him a filthy-minded little shit. He'd only wanted to make her proud of him.

He knows now, however, that even if he'd succeeded in telling her, it wouldn't have changed anything. He'd still have been a little shit to her. She called him that with the frequency other people say honey or sweetheart; it was the opposite of a term of endearment, if there is such a thing. It also had an aptness he didn't understand until much later, though he'd been given a strong clue.

On one of his boredom-relieving strolls through the nursing-home halls he'd overheard two aides talking. "She acts so high and mighty," one of them said, "but she'd still be emptying bedpans if she hadn't let old Dent into her pants." They were obviously discussing his mother. She never wore pants, but she did order people around, and Mr. Dent, the owner of the nursing home, spent a lot of time with her. They often had meetings in the evening. Fat, pointy-nosed, wheezy Edward Dent, who hardly ever spoke to him, paid his tuition when he went to the university, by which time he'd figured out about the pants and the meetings. In a period spanning his freshman and sophomore years, Mr. Dent became a widower, married Momma, bought her an enormous new house in a gated neighborhood, and died of a heart attack. Momma inherited the nursing home over the protests of Mr. Dent's grown children and ran it until she died four years later. That's when he made his discovery. She'd told him his father was a no-good bastard who'd run off never to be heard from again, but going through her records he came across his birth certificate and saw Edward A. Dent in the space for father.

So he was a little shit, an embarrassing little turd his mother had shat out in order to gain power over her employer. And once she'd shat him out, she found another use for him; she chose his career and planned to put him in charge of finances at the nursing home after he got his MBA. If the police hadn't shut the home down when they did, he might have gone to jail for her. No doubt she was setting him up as a potential scapegoat.

He has to give her credit, though, for refusing to be just a rich man's whore. She wasn't after the money alone; she wanted authority and control. And despite her lack of a college education, she knew how to run a business. But her greed overwhelmed her ambition, and it would have cost her everything if a blood vessel hadn't burst in her brain.

Sometimes he wonders whether she willed her own death. But if she wanted to die, she showed no sign of it the last time he saw her. When he got word of her arrest, he drove straight from College Park to the police station in Frederick. They told him she'd been released on bail, and he found her at the house, having a drink and a cigarette on the white sofa in the huge, high-ceilinged living room.

Not yet forty-two, she was still beautiful, her hair and makeup perfect, her long legs elegantly crossed, her chestnut hair delicately silvered. He asked her what he could do to help. "What can you do?" she said, wisps of cigarette smoke curling from her rouged lips. "Keep your mouth shut, you little shit. That's what you can do."

Sticking the hairbrush in his pocket, he looks through the dresser drawers, taking the most time with the underwear drawer. She favors white bras and panties, not very sexy of her. But at the bottom there's a pair of black lace panties. He holds them up and exchanges a wry look with the good-natured handyman in the mirror. Then he walks over to the bed. He opens the toolbox and gets out the nylon cord. He measures a length from the top of a bed leg to the corner of the bed, cuts it three feet longer than that, makes a slip noose at one end and ties the other around the leg. Perfect. He does the same with three other lengths.

There's one more little job to do before he decides on his point of attack. He kneels beside the bed and lays out the things he's collected. He arranges them in order of use, but the order isn't set in stone. He's willing to let the moment dictate the action, and he has a feeling that with her he'll be less structured than usual. He'll regain the spontaneity of the throat-cutting episode. As he's anticipating the freedom and the power he'll feel, something makes him look up. There's a big man in a brown suit in the doorway, pointing a gun at him.

"Stand up," the man says, "and keep your hands away from your body."

It's as if he's slipped into a dream.

"Up," the man says.

It's no dream. But who is this man? A security guard? He looks familiar somehow.

The man steps toward him and pushes the hard muzzle of the gun against his forehead. "I won't tell you again," he says.

He stands, trying to think what to say. "I'm just here to fix—"

"Shut up. Turn around and put your hands on the wall."

He does as he's told. He feels hands patting him, reaching into his pocket and taking his keys. It comes to him where he's seen this man: in the background of the press conference. He remembers a large body in a brown suit. Not a security guard, then, but an actual policeman.

"Don't move," the man says.

He senses the man moving away. He's younger and quicker; he could run for it. But there's the gun.

"Hands behind you," the man says.

Cold metal encircles his wrists. The man moves away again, and he tries to think. He put those things on the floor, true enough, but he hasn't done anything with them. He could say it was all a joke, that he got the idea when she interviewed him. They'll look in his apartment, of course; but he's sure they won't find anything. And even if they learn about the house, he's been very careful there, as far as evidence is concerned. So he could still be all right. The burden of proof is theirs. The main thing now is to ask for a lawyer when they begin to question him. He's seen enough crime shows to know that this is what you do. He doesn't have a lawyer, but he can get one out of the phone book, and if he doesn't like him, he can get another one later on.

"Okay, let's go," the man says.

The gun barrel jabs him in the side and pushes him toward the bedroom door. They go through it and out the patio door and down the grass strip. He thinks about running again, but he's still afraid of the gun, and now he's handcuffed. The man prods him through the gap between the buildings to a car, opens the passenger door, and tells him to get in. He looks at him through the window. "Try anything," he says, "and I'll shoot you."

The man is carrying, he sees, the toolbox. He watches him go around and put it on the backseat, setting it beside a bottle in a narrow brown bag. And when the man climbs in, he smells liquor on his breath. Something to tell a lawyer. Or maybe something he could use now, since it indicates a lack of professionalism.

"It was just a joke," he says. "I thought of it when she was asking me about the missing woman. I wanted to see what the news did with it, that's all. I know it was silly and stupid of me, but I didn't mean any harm. So I'm wondering if we could come to some sort of an understanding."

"How much you got in your wallet?"

"My wallet? I left it in my…"

"No wallet, huh? Too bad."

Is the man toying with him? And if he is, could this mean he doesn't regard the crime as serious? Really, who would? Laws may have been broken, but nothing that warrants real jail time. Or any jail time. Maybe community service will be the extent of his punishment. He'll probably lose his job, but he'll want to move on anyway, after he's put in his hours serving slop to the homeless or whatever. He'll need a fresh start.

But they don't seem to be going downtown, where both the police and the sheriff's offices are located.

"Where are you taking me?" he says.

Silence. He feels a prickle of fear. Is the man driving him to some deserted spot to beat a confession out of him? A coerced confession, he also knows from TV, is inadmissible in court. So even if he says something to keep from being hurt, he should be all right. But the thought of this big man punching him, smashing him in the face, is terrifying.

He sees now they're on the road to North Hill. Maybe they're going to the police station there, although he isn't sure why they would be, except that North Hill is where the press conference was held. But this gives him hope he won't be hurt.

Then halfway to North Hill, the car turns into a dirt road bounded by trees.

"I don't understand," he says.

More silence. His uneasiness transforms into dread. The car stops, and the man comes around and pulls him out.

"It was just a joke," he repeats, ducking his head.

The man turns him toward the bright woods. He hears a car door open and close, sees a few leaves sail away on a breeze. A band of tape descends past his eyes and presses against his lips, pulling his head back. His knees wobble.

"Stand up," the man says.

The man guides him to the back of the car, opens the trunk, and tells him to get in. He climbs in, and the man puts another pair of handcuffs on his ankles and shuts the lid. Lying in the cramped dark, he feels the car begin to move. He hasn't been hurt, he realizes; these are merely scare tactics. But he isn't so scared that he won't ask for a lawyer. His cuffed hands are sweaty inside the rubber gloves, and he occupies himself for a while peeling the gloves off.

The car finally stops and he waits to be taken into the station, but the trunk stays closed. After a few minutes, the car starts up again. It keeps going and going, so long that he loses track of time. He gives in to the feeling that this is a dream, and then an actual dream, or a vision, blossoms in the dark. His mother is sitting at her dressing table, brushing the hair she's pulled over her bare shoulder. The rest of her hair flows down her pale, intricately wrought back. He can see all of her spine and the naked flare of her hips above the pink panties. Any second she'll glimpse him in the mirror and get up to punish him. But this doesn't happen. Somehow the dream has stopped itself there. He watches her slender upper arm, the elbow extended, moving a little as she brushes her hair.

The car slows and turns, rocking him, and stops. He hears the door click open and a distant rumbling, like a garage door going up. The car door shuts with a thunk, the car moves and stops again; the engine dies. Another click, more rumbling. This is it, he thinks, whatever it is. He shuts his eyes tight against the opening of the trunk. But nothing happens. More time passes, he doesn't know how long. He tries to summon the memory of his mother, but there's only the darkness. Music breaks out from somewhere and suddenly grows louder. The trunk lid flies up.

"These little ones for the cuffs?" the man says, holding out his key ring.

He nods.

The man reaches in and unlocks the cuffs around his ankles. "Get out," he says.

He climbs out and sees that he guessed right; he's is in a garage. In front of the car there's a silver-knobbed door with a shovel and a folded blue tarp beside it. His own garage, he realizes. "Lights will guide you home," someone is singing.

The man pushes him toward the door, and they enter the kitchen and the roaring furnace of the music. Night shows between the window curtains. They go through the kitchen to the dining room, where the blasting radio sits on its chair next to the basement doorway. They go past it down the basement steps, the man closing the door behind them. He sees that the bed and the cheval mirror have been pulled out from the wall, and the bed is draped in a plastic drop cloth and surrounded by other cloths on the floor. It's a horrifying sight. The man has worked it all out.

"I'm guessing the mirror goes behind the head," the man says. "It's the logical place."

"Those are just some things I store here," he says.

The man shoves him hard onto the bed facedown, takes off the handcuffs and flips him over on his back. Instinctively, he springs up, but a horrible stinging pain in his throat drops him, and while he's immobilized the man slips his hands through looped ropes tied to the bed.

Showing him the stun gun, the man says, "Never tried one of these before. Does most of the work for you, doesn't it?" The man grabs his ankles and ties them to the bed too. "Now I'm gonna take the tape off, but you know there's no point in yelling for help. Door's shut and the radio's turned up. The way you do it, right?"

The man comes round to his face and pulls out a pocketknife. He slips the blade under the tape, cuts upward, and rips it off.

"It isn't what you think," he tells the man in a rush, feeling blood trickle down his jaw. "It's a game. I do it with prostitutes. No one gets hurt."

The man doesn't seem to hear. He removes his coat and lays it on the long sink cabinet. He looks at the tools on the pegboard above the cabinet, takes down the hedge clippers, and carries them over to the bed.

"I saw your special shelf of knives and whatnot. So I figure these clippers and the other tools you've got hanging up are just for show, to make the basement look normal."

"Yes. I mean, I use those tools as anybody would. And I swear I've never used anything down here to harm anyone. At her apartment, it was all a—"

The man opens the clippers and catches the index finger of his right hand between the blades. He tries to jerk his finger away, but the blades tighten and cut into the flesh.

"You want to keep your finger," the man says, "you need to tell the truth."

"Please," he says. "I haven't done—"

Incredibly, the shears snap shut on his finger. He screams and closes his eyes, seeing in his mind steel severing white bone. When he looks again, the finger is a gushing stump.

"Oh, God!" he cries.

"Tell me."

"Please! I'm a banker, not a criminal!"

The man cuts off another finger.

"All right!" he screams. "I brought some women here!"

"What did you do to them?"

"I can't remember. It—it was like being in a trance."

"Try," the man says, and cuts off another finger.

Sobbing, he feels his bowels give way.

"Jesus Christ! What a stink," the man says. He puts the blades around the thumb of the bleeding hand. "You want this thumb?"

"I tied them up," he says. "I had sex with them."

"You didn't have sex with them, you sick fuck. You raped them."

"Yes."

"What else did you do to them?"

"I made them say things."

"What things?"

"That… I was their master, their God, they belonged to me."

"You pathetic bastard. What else?"

"Then I killed them."

The shears dig into his thumb.

"But first I cut them. I shocked them. I burned them. I stuck things inside them."

The man is silent for a time. At last he says, "And you watched yourself do it in the mirror."

"Yes."

"How did that feel?"

"It's a compulsion. I can't help myself."

The shears snap off the thumb.

"Please, please, let me go!" he sobs. "Take me to the police station! I'll confess everything!"

"You'll confess it here, first," the man says.

Then there's still hope. The man is a crazed, vicious drunk, but he intends to take him in. Maybe he'll let him pick up his fingers too. They could be reattached. He nods, whimpering.

"Tell me about your last victim," the man says.

"She—I got her when she came out of her office."

"You mean the grocery store, don't you?"

He looks at the man. "Yes. I forgot. I stunned her and put her in the trunk and brought her here."

"Did she say anything, other than what you forced her to?"

"She said what they all say."

"*Tell me.*"

"*She pleaded with me to let her go. She said there were people who loved her. She begged me not to hurt her. Then she begged me to stop. She called for her mother.*"

The man lowers the shears. "*How did she die?*" *he says in a soft, almost inaudible voice.*

"*I strangled her.*"

"*Where's her body?*"

He takes a chance that the man won't search for it until after he's driven them to the station. "*West of town,*" *he says.* "*There're some woods behind a boarded-up old house. I buried them all there.*"

The man stares down at him. His eyes are like polished black pebbles.

"*I've told you everything,*" *he sobs.* "*Please take me in now.*"

"*Take you in where?*"

"*To the police station.*"

"*Why would I do that?*"

"*It's your job.*"

"*No, it isn't. Used to be, but not anymore.*"

He shuts his eyes and sees his mother brushing her long brown hair. It looks so soft and shiny against her naked back. He feels hands at his pants, unbuckling and unzipping them, yanking them down. His mother sees him in the mirror. She turns and stands. She marches toward him on her long white legs, her breasts shaking. Her hand grips the brush.

"*Momma!*" *he cries.*

Chapter 17

Halfway down the stairs she saw Fallon off to one side facing away from her. He must have heard her, but he gave no sign. He was standing at the foot of a bed. She moved closer and saw the thing his broad back had screened—the spread-eagled corpse of a man.

The man was dressed in blue working clothes, so for a moment she didn't recognize him as Middleton. His arms and legs were tied to the bedposts. His bloody right hand seemed to be missing most of its fingers. His open eyes had an inward expression, and his lips were slightly parted, as if he were about to speak. Not a big man, he looked like a child with Fallon looming over him. There was an entry wound in his right temple, and a spray of gore fanning from the left temple across the plastic sheeting on the mattress. She forced her eyes lower to what they'd shied away from: his pulled-down pants and the pulpy, blood-drenched pubis where his genitals had been.

She pushed the muzzle of her gun into Fallon's back. "Don't move," she said, and slipped his gun from the holster.

"Just going to clean up," he said.

She checked the safety, put his gun in her pocket, and pulled out her cuffs.

"Hands behind you."

Meekly, almost absent-mindedly, he offered her his hands. His rolled-up sleeves were stained red.

From somewhere above came a loud pounding followed by a crash.

She unclipped her badge and held it up.

"Down here!" she called.

Several uniforms came rumbling down the stairs with their guns drawn.

"Holy shit," one of them said.

"Westbrook, Virginia county sheriff's office," she said, and gestured toward Fallon. "I just cuffed him for the murder."

"Murder ain't the half of it," another one said.

"The victim could be a serial killer," she said. "So this room, this house, is potentially a multiple crime scene."

"I know that voice," someone said above them. She turned and saw a middle-aged, pot-bellied man descending the stairs. He had on a porkpie, a cheap blue suit, and a crooked grin. The grin faded as he reached the bottom and took in the carnage. But it reappeared when he looked at her.

"Detective Westbrook, I presume," he said.

"Detective Decker."

"Heard some Virginia cop was calling for backup and thought it must be you." He looked her up and down. "Little taller than I imagined, but otherwise you're in the ballpark." He pointed his chin toward the corpse. "This the guy we were talking about?"

"Yeah."

He walked around the bed, put on a rubber glove, stooped, and came up holding a pair of bloody garden shears. "Ouch," he said. "So you think the vic's a serial killer?"

"He could be."

"He confessed," Fallon said in a slurred voice.

She and Decker exchanged glances. Despite Fallon's drunkenness, this might stand as an admission of guilt.

"Well, I'd probably confess too," Decker said, "if you'd done some pruning on me. Who are you, anyway?"

"Her uncle."

"The last victim's uncle," Cynthia clarified. "His name's Michael Fallon. He's a retired cop, Baltimore homicide."

"Cop, huh?" Decker said.

"They must do interrogations different in *Ballmore*," one of the uniforms said.

"Maybe they should call it *Ball-less*," another said.

Decker cast a cold eye on the uniforms. "Didn't you comedians hear the detective? We might have more than one crime scene here. Everybody out. And post a man in the yard."

When they'd gone, he put the shears down and said, "How come you didn't give me a heads-up about your little night visit?"

She explained as best she could.

"Okay, Sherlock," he said. "Wouldn't have believed it myself, either. You got the gun that made those holes in the vic's head?"

She pulled it out of her pocket, and he came around and took it from her and laid it on the end of the mattress, between Middleton's spread legs. Then he turned Fallon around, and she saw the coppery web of blood on his pants and shirt.

"Mr. Fallon," Decker said, "you're now officially under arrest in the great state of Maryland."

He called the ME on his cell, and the three of them went up the stairs, Fallon first.

Her lingering state of hyper-alertness lent the ride downtown a dreamlike intensity. Overhead, the streetlights swam by like golden jellyfish, their slow passage in synch with Decker's off-key humming of "Strangers in the Night." At the station, Decker handed Fallon over to the cop in charge of booking, telling him to bag Fallon's pants and shirt as evidence. He got her a cup of coffee and introduced her to the detective who would take her statement.

"How she ended up here is sorta complicated," he said to the man, whose name was Greenberg. "But I think you could boil it down to she learned a couple things that roused her suspicions. How's that, Detective Westbrook?" She nodded her assent. "Good," he said. "I'll leave you guys to it."

Two hours later she read and signed the statement Greenberg had prepared, and it was only then that it occurred to her to inform Roger. She had to wake him up, which maybe accounted for his difficulty in grasping the story. "Jeff told you what? *Your* apartment? Who's Middleton again? You went where? What's Fallon got do with— Cut off his what? Jesus!" When at last he began to put things together, his tone became more guarded, as if he didn't know whether his official attitude should be praise or disapproval. Finally, he said, "Guess I'd better come. Where are you again?"

She put her cell away and leaned back in her chair, and the next thing she knew somebody was shaking her shoulder. She opened her eyes on Decker grinning at her.

"Your guy's on his way," he said. "He called for directions."

"Thanks."

"Want to hear about my little chat with Fallon?"

"Sure."

"Once we got some coffee in him, he was the model suspect. Waived his rights and laid it all out. Said he'd followed you and your partner around, then gone back to the places you'd been, pretending to be a cop. Didn't suspect Middleton of anything; just wanted to talk to him. Middleton wasn't at the bank, so he went to his apartment and didn't find him there either. Then he drove to a house you'd gone to."

"Friend of the last victim."

"Well, nobody was there, either. He went back to his motel and finished off a bottle, which necessitated a trip to the ABC store. After that he decided to try Middleton's apartment again. Still nobody there. He waited a while, and he was about to leave when a car pulled into Middleton's spot. The driver gets out carrying a shopping bag and a toolbox and goes up to the apartment. Fallon's cop instinct kicks in. This seems a little hinky for a sick banker, so he waits some more, and a few minutes later Middleton comes racing down in work clothes and a baseball cap—more hinky yet—and gets back in his car. Fallon followed him to your place, not knowing it was yours, and saw him go around back. He went around too and monitored the break-in, saw there wasn't anybody home. After a little bit, he went in and caught Middleton laying out stuff in your bedroom. That's also when he noticed your academy diploma on the wall. He cuffed him with some cuffs he found in the toolbox—which reminds me..."

Decker pulled a pair of handcuffs from his coat pocket and gave them to her. "Wouldn't want you to have to reimburse the sheriff's office. Anyway, he drove them somewhere secluded, gagged Middleton, and stuck him in the trunk. Then he went to Middleton's apartment and got lucky. Thinking, like you did, that it wasn't the ideal place to take victims, he used Middleton's mailbox key to check his mail and found a bill for a Frederick address from a lawn-mowing outfit. The rest of the story you know."

"Did Middleton tell him what he did with the bodies?"

"Dumped in a wooded area west of town. Or so Middleton said."

"You think he lied?"

Decker shrugged. "Maybe, if he still had hopes of getting out of there alive. But after the second or third finger..." An odd look crossed his face.

"What?"

"Fallon was sorta apologetic about relieving Middleton of his manhood. Said he shot him to put him out of his misery. Buyer's remorse, I guess."

"Doesn't change anything," Cynthia said.

"No. One more thing. Fallon was a little fuzzy on the time line, but I estimate he finished up with Middleton between six and seven p.m., before you called me. M.E.'ll probably let that stand."

"It could have been later."

"Take what you can get, is my philosophy."

Five minutes later Roger arrived accompanied by Rick. Decker filled them in on Fallon and added, looking at her, "You got a helluva detective here." She wondered if Fallon had told him she'd been pulled off the lead.

Roger didn't seem to hear. "Lemme get this straight," he said. "Fallon crapped up two of Middleton's crime scenes. So we could still be up shit creek."

"Look on the bright side," Decker said. "The perp's dead."

"Yeah, but I want this case to be dead too."

"There's the body dump, if that pans out," Cynthia said. "And Middleton's car should be in my apartment parking lot."

"There you go," Decker said.

"Also," Cynthia said, "He might have kept trophies." She told Roger about the missing purse of the Frederick murder victim.

"So you wanna toss his place?" Decker said.

"Might as well," Roger sighed.

"That's the spirit," Decker said.

Decker and Greenberg led the way in their car, and she rode with Roger and Rick. They searched the house for signs of previous murders and anything that might be a memento—purses, panties, a piece of jewelry, photographs, a videotape. They worked fairly quickly because there was so little in the way of furnishings. The one bedroom with something in it contained a covered mattress and a few clothes hanging in the closet. The bathroom had essential toiletries and a couple of towels; the kitchen, a few dishes and utensils; the dining room, the table and the radio. Otherwise, there was nothing above ground.

The small basement, brightly lit by two bulbs in a suspended socket, was of greater interest. Middleton's corpse had been removed, but the bloody drop cloth still covered the bed, and there were other blood-spattered drop cloths on the concrete floor, on one of which lay the garden shears. A cheval glass stood behind the bed. She'd noticed it before, but only now did its purpose register. Against one wall there was a long cabinet with a sink in the middle. A stun gun, Fallon's suit coat, and the toolbox he'd mentioned to Decker lay on top of it.

The toolbox was open, revealing a rubber mallet, duct tape, a knife, rubber gloves, and condoms. They looked in the cabinet and found two shelves whose contents added to the story of Middleton's victims. The lower one was stocked with several bottles of bleach, unopened packages of drop cloths, a box of rubber gloves, linked packets of condoms, a box of energy bars, and a thick coil of nylon cord. The upper one held an assortment of knives, two kinds of pliers, a screwdriver, empty soda bottles, a cattle prod, and a blowtorch. But there were no trophies. And given all the signs of meticulousness, maybe no trace evidence, either.

Around five Decker called the techs and gave them some instructions, and they went to an all-night diner he knew. Cynthia followed in her car, which she'd left on Middleton's street. Breakfast was quiet. Even a hard case like Decker seemed to have been affected by the implications of what they'd seen. Cutting his pancakes he muttered, "Energy bars. Son of a bitch." When they parted in the restaurant parking lot, he said to her, "It's been a kick, detective. I'll be waiting for that call."

"What call?" Roger said as Decker walked away.

"Phone sex," Cynthia said.

"Phone— oh, it's a joke, right?"

"You up for searching Middleton's apartment?" she said.

Roger took a moment to engage the question. "Uh, yeah. Be good to do it before we see Sampson."

"Want to do it now?"

"Let's say two hours. I'll get the warrant."

She drove to her apartment and scanned the parking lot for unfamiliar cars. At the end of the building there was a black Taurus she didn't remember. She phoned in the license number, got a confirmation it was Middleton's, and tried the doors. They were locked, but she could do a search later. The Taurus wasn't going anywhere. She glanced at her watch. Plenty of time to freshen up.

But when she opened her front door, her heart went into overdrive. An air of menace suffused the place. She felt as if someone were about to leap out at her from every hiding place, and even more irrationally, that the apartment itself was a giant trap waiting to snap shut on her. She fought her panic long enough to shower and change, and then she went to the station and busied herself until Roger and Rick were ready to go.

Unlike the sepulchral house in Frederick with its tidy torture chamber that didn't bear thinking about, Middleton's apartment gave off a sense of ordinary life, of meals cooked, laundry folded, TV watched. A few paperbacks, most of them thrillers, lay stacked on a lamp-table shelf. But the longer she was in it, the less persuasive this atmosphere felt. The place reminded her of a stage set. The only thing that seemed real was a room with barbells, a weight rack, and a treadmill.

She could imagine him watching himself in the mirror on the closet door, just as he'd watched himself in the basement mirror. His life had been a hall of mirrors reflecting only himself and, indistinctly, fleetingly, his victims. Without them, it would have been a sad waste of consciousness. With them, it was a horrific paradox: an insect-like constriction of behavior, concerned solely with its own satisfaction, had generated endless shock waves of grief and anguish. Evil might still be a necessary word, as Jack Slaughter had said, but she didn't think Middleton had been capable of appreciating the evil he'd done, was still doing. He'd been conscious of the suffering he inflicted, of course, but in an external way. He couldn't identify with it; he couldn't imagine it as his own. Or maybe that *was* the nature of evil.

On the bedroom wall there was a framed photograph of an attractive, thirty-something brunette with prominent cheekbones, alert brown eyes and a bland smile. His mother, she guessed. It was the kind of picture that people had made for business purposes. Maybe it had hung in the lobby of the nursing home. To have put it in here, where he could see it when he went to bed, Middleton must have loved his mother in some way, even if he'd devoted his life to killing women who resembled her.

"Definitely doable," Rick said, staring at the picture.

"Who isn't, according to you?" Cynthia said.

"Hey, I've got my standards. Nobody with a walker."

They started their search in the bedroom and moved on to the other rooms. They looked in all the dresser drawers, and also behind and under them. They looked under the bed and between the box springs and the mattress. They went through the closets and unscrewed the faceplates of the outlets and the grid over the vent. They opened every bottle in the medicine chest, looked between the towels and sheets in the linen closet, and took the lid off the toilet tank. They went through a filing cabinet in the exercise room and spent a considerable amount of time in the kitchen. They probed the living-room sofa and unzipped the cushion covers and felt the carpeting along the edges for lumps. Nothing.

After two hours, Roger said, "Okay. Let's hope the techs come up with something."

"Just a minute," she said.

She went back into the bedroom, took the picture off the wall, and turned it over. Metal clips held the cardboard backing in place. She depressed the clips and removed the cardboard, and there against the underside of the mat were four plastic baggies, one on top of the other, each containing a thin tangle of brown hair strands.

By this point Roger and Rick had come into the room.

Remembering her hairbrush on the floor with the torture kit, as well as the missing purse of the Frederick victim, she said, "These pieces of hair may have come from brushes, so there could be follicles and DNA."

"Bingo," Rick said.

"Was Fallon ever in this apartment?" Roger said.

"He told Decker he checked the mailbox," Cynthia said, "but that's downstairs."

"Then we just caught a break," Roger said. "Let's go see Sampson."

Chapter 18

Sampson, sitting behind his desk, listened to Roger, but after a minute or two he stopped him and began to ask Cynthia questions, taking notes on her answers. When he finished his interrogation, he put down his pen and steepled his fingers.

"Congratulations," he said to her.

"Thank you, sir."

"But most of it was just hunches, not real police work. You got lucky."

Meaning, she thought, her woman's intuition had gotten lucky. "Yes, sir," she said.

"That's why I'm not suspending you for not communicating your suspicions to the Maryland police. Even though if you had, Middleton might be telling us things we won't find out any other way."

She nodded. He was right about the missed opportunity, or the chance of a missed opportunity, depending on when Middleton had died. But she suspected that his leniency had an ulterior motive.

"Still, we've got enough to hold a news conference. I'm calling one for two p.m. in North Hill. We'll meet back here at one-thirty."

There it was: the desire to shine untarnished.

She left Rick dozing in his chair and Roger looking sulky, his bottom lip stuck out more than usual, and drove herself to a nearby bookstore and from there to the hospital. Jeff was awake and alert, talking to his mother and Denise Johnson.

"You remember Denise," Jeff said.

"I do. Hello."

Denise smiled at her.

"This is all her fault for having lunch with me," Jeff said. "Otherwise, I would've seen Freddy sooner and missed the chase."

"Well, thank you very much," Denise said.

"But I'll forgive her if she treats me to dinner some time."

"Don't press your luck," Denise said.

"So the surgery went well?" Cynthia said.

"I'm still here."

"Hush," Mrs. White said. "It went just fine."

"Good." She opened the bag she was carrying and took out the books in it, soft-cover editions of *Alice in Wonderland* and *Paradise Lost*.

"Something to occupy your time," she said, handing them over.

"Gee, um, thanks," Jeff said. "Will there be a test?"

"No test. The Alice book is really two books, by the way. The second one's called *Through the Looking Glass*."

"I've learned something already. Okay, then. Any news?"

"Yep. Quite a lot."

"Oh, yeah? Shoot."

Mrs. White stood. "I'll be down the hall. You can come too, Denise."

"Actually, Denise is part of the story," Cynthia said.

"I am?"

Mrs. White stopped but remained on her feet, ready to flee, and Cynthia launched into her tale once again. When she got to Middleton, Denise said, "I knew it! I knew something was off about that man." And despite her omission of the most horrific details, Mrs. White kept exclaiming, "Lord have mercy!" and shaking her head as if to dislodge the memory.

Jeff, who'd listened intently, said, "Now that, ladies, is how it's done. No chasing after wild theories. Just following the facts."

Cynthia laughed. "Sampson said pretty much the same thing, without the irony."

"I'm glad my influence is rubbing off."

"Couldn't have done it without you."

"You mean, without knowing what I got from Denise," Jeff said. "Maybe Denise should be a cop."

"No, thank you," Denise said.

"More exciting than counting money."

"Chasing people through the woods and looking at dead bodies is excitement I can do without."

"Amen, child," Mrs. White said.

Cynthia told them about the press conference and excused herself. Back at headquarters she found Roger and Rick lurking outside of Sampson's empty office. She lurked with them until Sampson showed up, his prematurely white hair freshly barbered. He grabbed a folder and they went down to the parking lot.

"Ride in back with me," he told her, and once they were underway he said, "When I finish talking, I'll introduce you to take questions. But remember, this is an on-going investigation. Don't add anything substantive. Also, we might have more media than last time. I indicated in the announcement that there'd been a break in the case."

The press was out in force all right, so many of them that the crowd had spilled over into the street, and the police had closed off the block. A uniform moved a sawhorse and let their car through. They went up to the portico as they'd done the last time. Precisely at two Sampson straightened his form-fitting, beribboned dress coat, led them down, and stepped to the microphone.

He referred to Cynthia as a member of the investigative team, creating the impression that she'd remained central to it, and presented a summary of events that began with the break-in at her apartment and ended with the discovery of the packets of hair. In passing, and without making a connection between them, he mentioned the time of her call to Decker and the "Frederick authorities'" estimate of time-of-death, which was Decker's. He also praised her "outstanding professionalism."

"Thanks to Investigator Westbrook and her team," he said, "we're confident that we've solved the three disappearances, and possibly an earlier Frederick homicide, although we'll have to wait on the DNA analysis of the hair to be positive. Now Investigator Westbrook will take your questions."

If her night ride through Frederick had seemed surreal, this experience was like a nightmare. Cameras flashed and whirred and shouts went up. The cacophony of voices resolved itself into questions about how she'd figured things out. She answered that she couldn't have done it without the help of her partner Jeff White, Detective Decker of the

Frederick police, and FBI profiler Jack Slaughter, and she explained why Jeff couldn't be there. Then came the fishing expeditions to which she responded with Roger's mantra of "I can't comment on that."

She thought she was lulling the media beast to sleep when suddenly it pounced. How did you feel, it asked, when you saw those things next to your bed? Had you met Fallon before? What did you think of him? Why did Middleton pick you? What was going through your mind when you broke into his house? Discovered the body? How long have you been with the sheriff's office? How tall are you? (laughter) Are you married?

Her brief answers unintentionally encouraged a rapid-fire assault that made her feel less and less in control of the situation, and by the time she was hit with the questions about her personal life, she was reeling. It was a great relief when Sampson took over. He announced that he'd requested a fast track for the DNA tests on the hair and would call another press conference as soon as the results were in.

When they got back in the car, Sampson said nothing, and Cynthia thought she must have made a botch of it. A few minutes into the ride he broke his silence. "A media event like this is good for the division," he said, "but we can't let it to turn into a circus. We need to put the victims and their families first. Understood?"

Was this really his concern, she wondered, *or was it the media interest in her?* But since she agreed with his point, and hated being in the spotlight, she said, "Yes, sir" along with Roger and Rick.

"So I'll do the talking to the press," he said.

"Yes, sir."

"A reporter wants to interview you, send him to me."

At headquarters he repeated his order before letting them go. She decided to work on her report, but checked her cell first. There were two voice messages.

The first was from Jeff: "Hey, team leader. You looked good, except for the fisheye thing. Just kidding. You were fine. Really. I hope that sounded sincere. Oh, and thanks for sharing the glory. My mom's been yanking nurses in here to look at Catwoman's sidekick."

The second was from Sally: "Honey! Maria had the little TV on in the kitchen, and she saw you! She said you solved the case! Good work! *Now* they know what they've got! Ask for a promotion!"

She did a rough of the report and stopped, too brain weary to continue. It was only then that she thought about going home. The prospect made her uneasy, and the feeling intensified as she drove there. When she entered her complex and saw the army of reporters camped at her door, she felt something akin to gratitude. Now she had a reason to stay away. A bearded photographer spotted her where she'd braked and began running toward the car. Behind him, the crowd roused itself and came running too, one of them sprinting past the photographer. She backed up, spun the wheel, and sped off. Several direction changes later, she turned into a restaurant parking lot and called Sally.

"A bunch of reporters have staked out my place," she said. "Could I stay with you tonight?"

"Honey, you already know the answer to that. The guest room's yours whenever you want it."

She arrived close to seven. Sally served Maria's frijoles and chiles rellenos and opened a bottle of champagne to celebrate the victory. After they'd clinked glasses, Sally said, "Now tell me what you can." Cynthia did, going into more detail than she had with Mrs. White and Denise, while Sally listened in clamped-mouth silence. When she finished, Sally said, "Thank goodness for Mr. Fallon."

It was something that had crossed Cynthia's mind too. "Yeah. He may have saved my life. Too bad instead of calling the cops he ruined his own."

Sally shook her head. "Old as I am, it never ceases to amaze me what human beings are capable of. On the whole I prefer the company of horses—present company excepted, of course." She looked at Cynthia. "Are you all right?"

"Yes."

"You sure?"

"I was just thinking about my apartment. I wasn't exactly disappointed that I couldn't stay there."

"And you never have to again, if you don't want to. You can stay here till you find some other place, or you can stay here period."

She appreciated the invitation, and thanked Sally for it. But she had to go back; if she didn't, she'd become part of Middleton's legacy.

While they were doing the dishes, her cell rang. The caller said, "Cynthia, hi, this is Amanda Swift, Fox News."

"Sorry," she said, glad for Sampson's order. "You need to speak to my division commander, Major Sampson."

"This isn't so much about the case. I want to do a personality profile of you."

"He'd still have to approve. But you don't need to ask him because I'm not interested."

"Oh, but our viewers are very interested in you. You should see the e-mails we've been getting, hundreds of them, ever since we showed the press—"

"Sorry. Goodbye." She hung up.

"Reporter?" Sally said.

"Uh-huh. Somebody must've leaked my number."

The phone rang again almost immediately, but this time it was Jeff. "Guess what?" he said. "I'm gonna be a TV star too. Channel 3 tonight at eleven."

"They interviewed you?"

"Yeah. About you. But don't worry, I didn't tell them anything."

"Thanks."

"No problem. I don't know anything to tell."

She hung up and the phone rang again, another reporter. She shut it off, but not before receiving a text message from a publisher: "Work with us on book. Opportunities unlimited. Movie rights, TV appearances, reality show, etc."

She and Sally passed the time until the news reading the Post. At five minutes before eleven, she awakened Sally, who'd fallen asleep in her chair, and turned on the TV. The disappearances were the lead story. The graying, helmet-haired male anchor somberly described their effect on the public and switched to a brighter tone: "But police say the reign of terror is over. Major Harold Sampson of the sheriff's office broke the news today in a press conference." This cued a clip of Sampson speaking, after which the anchor said to the young black woman beside him, "Just how they cracked the case is a remarkable story, isn't it, Britney?"

"Indeed it is, Don," said Britney. "Detective Cynthia Westbrook solved it almost single-handedly." She summarized Sampson's version of events, and then Cynthia saw herself on the screen fielding questions.

"There you are!" Sally said.

"Jeff was right, I do look fish-eyed," she said.

"No, you don't," Sally said. "You look fine."

Don, the male anchor, commented, "Some say the word 'hero' is overused these days, but there's no question it fits Detective Westbrook."

"Indeed," Britney said. "News at 11's Calinda Delgado has more on her."

The scene shifted to a young Hispanic woman standing in front of the lighted hospital. "Cynthia Westbrook's partner is Detective Jeffrey White," she said. "The information he uncovered led her to the alleged killer's house, but he was unable to make the journey with her. He broke his leg yesterday afternoon helping North Hill police pursue a suspect in a carjacking. Now, his leg was broken in several places, and he underwent surgery this morning at Harris County Hospital behind me. Earlier this evening I spoke with him and his mother."

The taped interview began. Jeff was sitting in the raised bed with his mother beaming beside him.

"Detective White," the reporter said, "how are you feeling?"

"Good, thanks."

"Mrs. White, you must be very proud of your son."

"I certainly am," Mrs. White said.

Holding the microphone toward Jeff, the reporter said, "How would you describe your partner Cynthia Westbrook?"

Jeff seemed to give it some thought. "Tall," he said.

"She sure is," Mrs. White said. "She's a lot taller than my boy."

Jeff jerked his thumb at his mother. "She likes to point that out, for some reason."

"What about the courage Detective Westbrook demonstrated?" the reporter said.

"She really kept her cool," Jeff said, "answering all those questions."

"I mean last night when she broke into the alleged killer's house alone."

"He was dead, wasn't he?"

"Yes, but his alleged killer wasn't."

"The alleged killer of the alleged killer. Sounds a little weird, doesn't it? But the one who's still alive confessed, so I think we can drop the *alleged* for him."

"Could you tell me more about your partner?"

"Well, she's sort of literary. In fact, this is what she gave me today." Grinning, he held up the two books with their covers facing the camera.

The live Calinda outside the hospital said, "In case you didn't catch those titles, they were *Paradise Lost* and *Alice in Wonderland*. Detective Westbrook isn't just a superb detective; she's also a very serious reader."

"*Paradise Lost*," Britney chuckled. "Not your typical beach book."

"But *Alice in Wonderland* is fun," Don said. "The Mad Hatter. The

White Rabbit."

"The Jabber-something," Britney said.

"*Wocky*, I believe. Or *wock*. Well. Calinda, I understand that Detective White just happened upon the police chase he joined."

"That's right, Don."

"No thought to his own safety."

"None at all."

"Another undeniable hero."

"Indeed."

Don looked into the camera with a slightly pained smile. "Feathers everywhere. A truck carrying live turkeys overturns on Interstate 66. More when we return."

Cynthia clicked off the TV, and Sally said, "So that's Jeff."

"Yep."

"He must be a lot of fun."

"That's what all the girls think," Cynthia said.

Chapter 19

The next morning, a Friday, Cynthia turned her cell on before going to work. She ignored the unknown callers, but on the drive in she saw Roger's name and answered.

"We, uh, got a situation here," he said. "There're about a hundred reporters outside waiting for you to show. Sampson doesn't want you to come in."

"I don't have to talk to them."

"Yeah, I know. Was up to me… But that's the message."

"So what am I supposed to do?"

"Take some leave, he says. You never do, so you must have plenty."

She decided not to argue with the messenger. She pulled over and phoned Sampson.

"This isn't negotiable," he said. "In fact, you should get out of town. They might come looking for you at your place."

To appease him she said, "They already have. They were there last night when I got home. I drove off when I saw them, and I'm staying with a friend."

"Okay. Good. Hang tight until you hear from Bullock. It shouldn't be long. Soon as there's a fresh piece of meat in the water, they'll forget about you."

She gave him the benefit of the doubt that *fresh piece of meat* was an indictment of the press rather than of her. "Hope you're right, sir."

"Wait for Bullock." He hung up.

On the positive side, she thought, she'd been meaning to spend more time with Sally. Also, she wasn't keen on going home until this feeling about it had passed. But as she started to reverse course, she remembered that she'd need some clothes and other things. She drove to her apartment half wishing she'd find reporters there to chase her away again. No one was around, however, and fighting her irrational panic, she packed a suitcase and threw a few toiletries into a plastic bag. She also checked the back door to see whether Mr. Luce had replaced the broken pane, as she'd asked him to do. Her finger touched new glass. It was a good sensation, but not good enough. Not yet.

When she got to the farm, she told Sally about Sampson's decree, changed into jeans, a sweatshirt, and sneakers, and over Sally's objections went to help Juan and Reggie. She mucked out stables, mixed up the supplementary feed, put hay in the outdoor feeding troughs, inspected the wooden fences for breaks, groomed a couple of horses, and wrapped a cut on a filly's leg. It wasn't the day she'd planned on, but it was enjoyable nevertheless. She'd forgotten the satisfactions of performing discrete tasks and working to the unhurried rhythms of changing light and shadow, the slow boil and drift of clouds. But her muscles were out of practice, and by nightfall they were aching.

She took a hot shower, which helped, and she and Sally ate the feast Maria had prepared for them. During the meal her muted cell began to vibrate on the table. She didn't answer the unfamiliar number, but later she checked her voice mail and found a message.

"Hi," the caller said. "This is Jack Slaughter, of the FBI Academy? I wanted to add my congratulations to everyone else's. Very impressive work. Yesterday must qualify as one of those better days. Oh, and thanks for mentioning me, but you shouldn't have. All the credit belongs to you. I'd actually intended to call you before the news broke, but when it did, I knew you'd have your hands full with reporters. I was going to ask you to have lunch with me this weekend, if that's even a possibility—I realize I don't know anything about your personal life. But in case you'd like to, my home number is…"

Sally came into the living room and stopped, but Cynthia motioned her forward.

"It's the profiler I saw at Quantico," she said.

"He sounds nice."

"He does, doesn't he? He asked me out to lunch."

"You going?"

"I don't know. Maybe."

"Well, if you're worried about reporters, you could have lunch here. Maria's made more than enough for the weekend, as usual. And I'll stay out of the way."

"You don't have to do that. I'd like you to meet him."

"If you invite him."

"Right."

"I think I'll get my bath now."

It was Sally's not-so-subtle way of encouraging her to return the call. After replaying the message, she did.

"Hi," she said, "this is—"

"Detective Westbrook," Jack Slaughter said.

"Cynthia," she said. "I'm staying with my friend Sally, to escape all those reporters you spoke of. She has a horse farm about fifteen miles south of Parkerville. Would you like to join us for lunch tomorrow?"

"Yes," he said. "I'd like that very much."

"Will you be coming from Quantico?"

"No, Alexandria."

She gave him the directions, and the next day he showed up at noon, with a bottle of white wine for Sally. His arched eyebrows and angular features struck her as less comical this time; his intelligence made them appealing. Over lunch he asked Sally how she'd gotten into the stable business.

"I've always loved horses," she said. "I had one as a child until my father gambled away the family fortune, and when I married, I got myself another one. That sparked my son's interest in riding, so we bought a second horse for him. Anyway, after my divorce, I looked around for something to do, and naturally I thought of horses."

"Was it difficult getting started?" Jack said.

"Oh, yes. If it hadn't been for Bill—Bill Townsend, Cynthia knew him—I'd never have made it. He was my stable manager. I learned most of the horse-care end of things from him."

"Your son must have approved of your new life."

An interesting remark, Cynthia thought. It wasn't strictly relevant. Had Jack noticed something in Sally's expression or tone when she referred to her son?

"I'm sure he would have," Sally said. "He passed away before I bought the land."

"I'm so sorry. Was it an accident?"

"Meningitis, his freshman year at UVA. Another boy died of it too. Bobby was on the equestrian team, and I saw him compete at Hollins only a few days before he... Time's a funny thing, isn't it? That was thirty-five years ago, but it still feels like yesterday. I can remember it so clearly, the long afternoon shadows and Bobby on Scout, his horse, going over the jumps."

Cynthia had never heard this story before. Jack was good at getting people to open up. She'd have to bear that in mind.

Sally smiled at them. "Well, if you two young people will excuse me, I have an errand to run."

In Sally's absence, Cynthia drove Jack down to the stables, introduced him to Juan and Reggie, and showed him the stallion recovering from laminitis. Stroking the horse's neck, she described the disease, an inflammation of the tissues around the coffin bone inside the hoof, and told him how serious it was and how difficult it could be to cure.

"You're a horse person too," he said.

"Just peripherally. Sally has a couple of retired hunters she lets me ride, but I haven't done that in a while."

"Was it an interest in horses that led to your friendship?"

"Nope. She gave me a job. Before that, I hadn't been around horses at all. Wanna see some more of the farm?"

His eyes briefly searched hers. "Sure."

They walked past the riding arena and one of the paddocks up to the cemetery. Together they examined the weathered headstones of the people who'd once farmed the land, three generations of Jarvises. The oldest had died at age eighty-six in 1951, the youngest at three in 1902. She showed him Bill's polished granite marker.

"He made himself the caretaker," she said. "Kept the weeds out, put wildflowers on the graves. Maybe he wanted to be buried here, I don't know. He never said, though he wouldn't have. But Sally thought it was the right place for him. Now she pays Juan and Reggie a little extra to look after it."

"You speak of him very warmly," Jack said.

"He was a good friend."

"Did you learn about horses from him?"

"Yeah. And other things too. He was a terrific rider, even at his age, and the right size for a jockey. I know he would've made a great jockey when he was younger, but as a black person of his generation, he had to settle for being an exercise rider. And yet he didn't complain about it, never brought it up. I don't mean that as any kind of political statement. I just mean he got on with his life."

"I understand," Jack said.

They strolled down the far side of the hill and stopped under an oak. The temperature was in the low fifties, cool enough that she'd kept on her windbreaker and Jack his gray pullover sweater, but after their walk it felt just right. Pale orange stalks waved above the green grass of the rolling meadow, and in the distance several horses were grazing near a line of yellow and red trees. Beyond the trees, the autumnal mountains carried lightly on their backs the moving mountains of white cloud.

Jack let out an audible breath. "Maybe I should work on a horse farm," he said.

"Maybe we all should," she said.

"What was Sally's life like before this?"

"Broker's wife in Arlington. High society, I gather."

"Quite a change. Did her son's death have anything to do with it?"

"From what she's said, I think in the beginning she saw the farm as a kind of memorial to him."

"And now?"

"I imagine it's still that, but it's also her life." She didn't feel she should mention the string of live-in boyfriends, who were links to the old life. "And now it's a memorial to Bill."

"And a port in the storm for you," he said with a smile.

"Yep. Ready to head back?"

As they walked to the barn, he said, "Sally's story about her son made me think of my daughter going off to college. Her first choice is Stanford, which is about as far away from her mother and me as she can get. I've talked her into applying to some state schools as backups, and I'm selfishly hoping she'll have to settle for one of them."

Was this a ploy to draw her out? She didn't think so. He'd taken her hints earlier. "I've forgotten your daughter's name," she said.

"Anna."

"Does she live with you?"

"She lives with her mother, but my apartment is only two miles from their house. So I've managed to see a little more of her than I might have otherwise. And sometimes I can lure her into spending the whole day with me. Ever been to Woodbridge?"

"Once or twice. Looks like it was built yesterday, but the bay, so-called, is nice."

"That's Woodbridge. Two years ago, I stopped there on the way home from the Academy. I ate at a restaurant and took a stroll on the boardwalk down to the marina. It was twilight, and the boats were tinged a kind of glowing violet. The water was the same color and absolutely still. You could see a perfect, upside-down marina in it, with evening stars under the masts. Suddenly I felt this strong desire to own a boat. I knew it wasn't really about that. I'd never had much interest in boating. It was about the fact that my wife had just married the man she'd replaced me with and now my daughter had a stepfather, which made me feel even further marginalized. What I wanted was the beautiful, perfect life this scene represented. But despite my self-analysis and my tendency to be cautious and deliberate—some would say boring—the next day I bought a middle-sized motorboat and rented a slip at the marina. And when after a few weeks I felt seaworthy, or river-worthy, I invited Anna to go boating with me. It turned out she loved being on the water, and so I had my lure."

"I'm glad it worked out."

"Yes. She might have hated it."

"Or you might have."

"I have to confess, I've never quite gotten past the symbolic value to real enjoyment. I like it best when she's along."

When they drove back to the house, Sally's pickup was there. Jack went in to say goodbye.

"Do you have to go?" Sally said. "I've got a new toothbrush, and I might even have some men's pajamas somewhere. You could sleep on the couch."

"I don't want to impose," Jack said.

"Would he be imposing?" Sally asked Cynthia.

"No," Cynthia said. "I'd like him to stay too."

"That makes it hard to say no," Jack said.

"Then don't," Sally said.

They spent the rest of the afternoon chatting in the living room and watching dusk descend on the meadowland outside the big window. At six she and Sally made a light dinner, which they ate on the tiled kitchen table. Then they moved back to the living room, taking their wine glasses and a new bottle with them. Jack asked about the psychology of horses, and while Sally discoursed on her favorite topic, fleshing it out with anecdotes, Cynthia drifted off on the couch. At some point she bobbed back into consciousness.

"…foster homes," Sally was saying. "She told me she lost count of how many."

"What about her family?" Jack asked softly.

"There was only her mother, I believe. She passed away, but that's all I know. Cyn's a private girl…"

Barely awake, her breathing still slow and deep, she felt caressed by these tender voices circling harmlessly the mystery of her past. She also felt a little guilty for eavesdropping. But before she could give them some sign she was awake, a yawn or a stretch, their voices dwindled to a soothing murmur, as if they were in a boat drifting away on the blackness. When at last she opened her eyes, moonlight bathed the room and there was a blanket over her.

Where was Jack? He'd been promised the couch. She became aware of a remote sighing behind her, and looking over the couch, she saw him lying on a mattress of blankets with an Afghan across his legs. He appeared to be wearing his own clothes rather than the judge's pajamas. His long, socked feet, sticking out from the Afghan, angled away from each other, and his face looked smooth and peaceful, and not at all comical. For a moment she considered letting his tidal breaths lull her back to sleep. But she needed to pee. She removed the blanket, slipped off her shoes, and tiptoed out of the room.

Chapter 20

They awoke to a heavy fog that dimmed the nearer countryside and hid the rest of it behind an opaline wall. Knowing Reggie and Juan would be delayed, Sally started out for the barn, and they went with her, their eyes on the muted red cross-stripes of her flannel overshirt. At the paddock fence a pair of horses, black and gray, stood shrouded in curling mist like icons of an equine religion. The fog had crept in through the open end-doors of the barn, and the lights, when Sally switched them on, gave off a murky glow.

Cynthia put a halter on the ailing stallion and led him into the corridor, where she hitched the cross ties to the hooks on either wall. Meanwhile, Sally and Jack had fetched muck rakes, a wheelbarrow, and some bags of shavings. Cynthia cleaned out the stall, shoveling the old wet shavings into the wheelbarrow and sifting the poop. She cut open a new bag of bedding and spread it over the rubber flooring. Then she cleaned and refilled the water bucket and led the stallion back in. She and Sally loosed the four other stabled horses into the paddock. Jack insisted on helping them muck out the stalls, and they let him work until the fog began to burn away, at which point Sally said, "Why don't you two go have some breakfast? The men should be along soon." As they were walking back to the house, Juan rumbled past in his old pickup and smiled his snaggle-toothed smile at them. She put on the coffee and started frying ham and eggs while Jack cleaned off his shoes in the mudroom. They had just finished eating when Sally returned. Jack thanked her and gave a goodbye hug, and Cynthia went with him out to his car.

"Still want to work on a horse farm?" she said.

"Theoretically."

"Theoretical horse poop does smell better."

He laughed. "I had a great time, the poop notwithstanding."

"Me too."

"Next weekend Anna and I are visiting those Virginia colleges she's not interested in."

"Well, maybe seeing them will change her mind."

"That's my hope. We may not get back until late on Sunday. Would you like to do something Monday evening, maybe have dinner?"

"Sure, if I'm not working a case."

"I'll call to see how things are."

"Or I'll call you."

He leaned forward as if to kiss her, but hesitated. She completed the action for him, kissing him lightly on the lips.

Over the next few days her body acclimated to the farm chores. Her muscles stopped aching, and she felt stronger and more supple, younger. The change added to the feeling of going back in time when she visited the cabin. She hadn't been inside it since Bill's death. There was a sitting room in the front where they'd watched TV, he in the black vinyl recliner where Sally had found him. The chair and the TV and the other furniture were gone, replaced by bags of pellet feed and horse bedding and other supplies. The two little bedrooms were empty, but the bathroom and the kitchen were still in use. The bathroom looked gas-station filthy, something Bill would never have tolerated. In the kitchen, a grimy percolator and two mugs with coffee rings in them sat on the counter, and a plastic ashtray full of cigarette butts adorned the dinette table.

She dumped the butts in the trashcan still under the sink, used a scrap of dishrag to wipe off the table, and sat down at it. Staring at the red and blue squiggles of the laminated surface, she thought of the meals she and Bill had shared here, and the tales he'd told her of his racetrack days, with an emphasis on the calamities. In his laconic way he could paint a vivid picture of horses colliding and jockeys being thrown and trampled. After dinner, they'd usually play a game of checkers. Part of his gamesmanship was to maintain a deadpan expression, but when she made an unwise move, the pipe in the corner of his mouth would lift a bit like an arrested exclamation mark. The checker box was the one thing of his she'd kept for herself. Sally had kept the pipe. There hadn't been much else in the way of personal belongings.

Years ago, before her time, Bill had nixed Sally's plan to build him a modest house, saying the cabin suited him just fine. Maybe he'd liked the snugness, or the simplicity of a compact existence. Reflecting on this, she felt an upwelling of grief, and then something else, a wild and dangerous longing. She got up and went outside.

Most of the time she didn't think about her job. Not being able to do it was frustrating, but it was also something of a relief, since her exile extended to her apartment. She hoped that by the time she went back to work, her problem would have solved itself. It seemed to be a weird variant of the adrenalin-fueled reaction she'd had to being shot at years ago.

A man she'd pulled over for speeding had leapt out of his car as she approached and pointed a gun at her. His shot missed, she ducked behind his trunk and drew her weapon, and her second round hit him in the chest, non-lethally as it turned out. She rushed over to him where he'd gone down, picked up his gun, and called for an ambulance. It was then that her hands started shaking so badly she had trouble opening her first-aid kit and staunching his wound. She didn't lose the shakes entirely for an hour or more, although by the time the M.E.'s and her backup arrived, she could hide them. But whatever the cause of her current reaction, there was no point in thinking about it until she had to.

She gave herself over to her self-imposed chores, the beauty of her surroundings, and her fascination with horses. She loved watching them trot across the meadow, their long legs dancing and their heads rhythmically dipping. Every step was charged with grace and power. Bill's first piece of advice had been to respect the power: *A horse might have a sweet temper, but he still a horse. You spook him, like you get behind him where he can't see you no more, and you can forget about that sweet temper, know what I'm saying?* Under his tutelage she'd learned to lessen the danger, as well as do the other things that put her in control of all that fluid strength.

On Wednesday, however, her mental vacation was interrupted by a phone call.

"Detective Westbrook," the caller said, "Thanks for the thanks."

"Detective Decker. You're welcome."

"You looked hot on TV."

"Despite my fishy stare?"

"Didn't notice it. Reason I called, other than to hear that voice, was to tell you we been searching the alleged dump site. Zippo. Either Middleton lied or Fallon was too drunk to get it straight."

The information gave her a funny feeling. "Thanks," she said. "I'm on leave, but I'll relay the message."

"Leave, huh? Your idea?"

"Nope."

"So they handed your case off to a deadbeat, and you solved it anyway, and now they won't let you be a rock star."

"That's not exactly fair to Roger—Lieutenant Bullock."

"Yeah, it is."

"And I don't want to be a rock star."

"No, you wouldn't."

"Where's Fallon now?"

"Hagerstown Correctional. Probably end up there after he's sentenced. I figure life without parole, for whacking Middleton's package off. But maybe he'll luck out and get a lady judge."

After she hung up, her brain wouldn't let go of the undiscovered dumpsite. If Middleton had lied about where it was, or its existence, maybe he'd lied about other things too. And this made her think of the unanswered questions in the Alicia Bradford case. Why had Alicia purchased a gun, and why hadn't they found it? Why had Middleton attempted two kills within two days of each other? There were also Jack's reservations about Alicia's youthful appearance and the Sunday timing of her abduction, too late to give Middleton very long with her—although he'd apparently been willing to settle for a few hours with his last would-be victim.

She had the nagging sense she was missing something. Not that it would matter when one of those pieces of hair was identified as Alicia's. Proof trumped complete understanding, an unattainable goal anyway. There were usually loose ends to a case, but if you could tie them all up, you still had to account for motive, which often came shaded with nuances and clouded by mysteries that resisted comprehension. Motives as presented in court were labels explained by other labels. Addiction/addictive personality. Jealous rage/PTS Disorder. Sadism/sociopathic behavior. The labels could be true as far as they went, but they were signposts on the edge of the forest.

On Sunday afternoon Roger called to say the coast was clear and to complain about the work piling up with her and Jeff both out. Full of conflicting emotions, she packed her things and said goodbye to Sally, who gave her an uncharacteristically hard hug.

"I've gotten used to having you around," Sally said.

"I'll try to come more often," she promised.

"You can bring Jack too—I mean, if you..."

"I know what you mean. You like having him around, too, don't you?"

Sally answered her question with a question: "He's good company, don't you think?"

Instead of going straight to her apartment, she visited Jeff at his mother's in the middle-class black enclave on the south side of Parkerville. Jeff took real pride in the neighborhood's origin as an encampment of escaped slaves during the Civil War. "What those folks did," he'd told her, "was put it on the Union boys. They were like, 'Okay, here we are. What ya'll gonna do about it?' That's where I get my proactive genes from."

He'd also told her that following the death of his father, a retired mail carrier, he and his five siblings had taken over the upkeep of the house so their mother could continue living in it on her bakery-shop wages. They were doing a good job, by the looks of it. The light blue siding and white shutters appeared to be freshly painted, and the ornamental shrubbery was well pruned. The house seemed too small, however, for a family of eight. She didn't see how it could have accommodated them unless the children had shared a single bedroom like Snow White's dwarfs. But the living room into which Mrs. White ushered her had a spacious feeling. No clutter, she realized. Minimum furniture, a few family pictures, a box of violets by the window. That was how they'd done it. Jeff's penchant for tidiness might have been born of necessity.

Jeff was in a wheelchair watching a football game on TV. When he saw her, he clicked off the TV and said, "Catwoman."

"Catboy," she said.

"Hmm. I may have to rethink that one. Sampson still pissed at you?"

"Watch your language," Mrs. White said.

He flashed a toothy smile. "Gee, it's great to be home."

"I'm starting back tomorrow," she told him. She noticed her get-well books on the coffee table and pointed to them. "Thanks, by the way, for telling the world who gave you those."

"No problem. Just my little contribution, you know, to your image. You been following yourself in the news?"

"Nope."

"Well, you're off the radar now, but for a few days there, thanks to me, you were 'the literary detective.'" He wiggled his fingers to signify quotes. "And 'the intellectual detective.' Which I think you'll agree is a *little* more dignified than the other stuff they were calling you: 'the tall, striking detective' and 'the sexy, cold-hearted detective.'"

"They didn't say that last thing," Mrs. White said.

"Sure they did. They got it from Roger." He rolled backwards and executed a wheelie. "Pretty good, huh?"

"Took him a whole afternoon to learn that," Mrs. White said. "He paid the neighbor boy to catch him."

"Hey, no giving away trade secrets," Jeff said.

"And now he's gonna bust his head showing off."

"Listen to your mother," Cynthia said. "You've only got the one head, and you need it to read *Paradise Lost*."

"Already did," Jeff said.

"Really?"

"Well, I skipped over some stuff, but I read the parts about Adam and Eve and the serpent. Didn't I, Mama?"

Mrs. White nodded.

"I tried to read it to her, but she didn't care for it."

"No, it's fine."

"She left the room."

"I just had some things to do."

He picked up the copy of *Paradise Lost*, flipped to the last page, and read aloud:

They hand in hand with wandering steps and slow,
Through Eden took their solitary way.

"Pretty cool ending," he said, "even if it doesn't rhyme."

From Mrs. White's Cynthia drove to the grocery store, and then, out of excuses, to her apartment. On the way she tried her old trick of diverting her attention from what she didn't want to feel or remember. She turned on the radio and found, by happy coincidence, the NPR short story program. Literature had always been her preferred method of self-distraction. Listening to an actor's spirited reading of *The Tell-Tale Heart*, she arrived home with her own heart beating calmly.

But things quickly became more difficult when she crossed the threshold. Through force of will she focused down on her domestic activities—putting the groceries away, making a sandwich, taking a shower—and managed to shrink her panic to a woozy feeling, like the first stage of the flu. She reduced it a bit more when she opened up *Mrs. Dalloway*, the book she'd been reading before she left. She finished it shortly after midnight and got in bed, expecting unconsciousness to release her from her struggle, and that's when the real trouble began.

Every time she felt herself sinking toward sleep, she'd snap awake, her heart lurching inside her chest like a trapped animal. She tried the couch with the same result. Around two she gave up and searched the bookcases for something else to read. The text from Dr. Ayers's class caught her eye. Its subject matter was twentieth century English poetry, arranged according to the poets' birth years. She started going straight through it: Housman, Yeats, Edwin Arlington Robinson, Walter De La Mare. After De La Mare came Robert Frost, and the last Frost poem was "Directive," the one Alicia had asked Walter Lewis about. She didn't think she'd ever read it. She would have remembered the first line: *Back out of all this now too much for us*. It was the beginning of a kind of spell, an incantation, to summon the past, and following it, Frost, or the speaker of the poem, as Dr. Ayers would have called him, to distinguish him from Frost the human being, guided the reader to the ruins of a village and gave the whimsical direction *pull in your ladder road behind you*. He then revealed a make-believe playhouse of shattered dishes under a pine, the nearby cellar hole of a house no longer standing, and a brook that had supplied water to it. The brook was his destination. There he produced a cracked goblet *like the Grail*, stolen from the playhouse, and gave a last directive that was as poignant in its way as the closing lines of *Paradise Lost*: *Drink and be whole again beyond confusion*.

Impossible to do, she thought. You could never again be the child you were and see life with innocent eyes. Frost would seem to agree. The poem's subtle air of posturing, the undercutting playfulness, the too assertive title, the imaginary nature of the journey, the crack in the drinking goblet—all of these signaled irony. Yet the irony co-existed with a heartfelt yearning for childhood's innocence and simplicity.

She thought of Alicia and her sister in their mother's drawing, Alicia in the paper sorcerer's hat and quilt robe. Her wooziness, she realized, was escalating into panic. She turned the page and concentrated on the more straightforward declarations of Carl Sandburg's "Chicago."

Chapter 21

At daybreak she fixed herself a pot of coffee and drank it all. She'd been in better shape, but going without sleep wasn't anything new to her; it came with the job. When she got to headquarters, Roger paired her with Rick, and they spent most of the day pursuing dead-end leads in a hair-salon robbery. They'd just ticked off the last of these when Jack called.

"Hi," she said, "You beat me to it. I'm in the western part of the county, investigating a robbery."

"So you're back at work. Good. If you aren't free tonight, I understand."

"No, we're about done here." She was also completely done in, but she wanted to see him, and besides, the alternative was staying at home.

They agreed to meet at a steak house they both knew in Manassas, a sort of halfway point. She arrived not long after he did, having spent as little time as possible in her apartment getting ready. When they were seated she asked him about his weekend with his daughter.

"She didn't like any of the colleges," he said. "She was sure they were far inferior to Stanford, which she hasn't seen yet."

"At least you got to spend some time with her."

"Yes, when she wasn't texting her friends. How about you? How was your day?"

"No arrests, but it was good to be out there again." She could feel the fatigue gathering behind her eyes.

"Are you all right?" he said.

"Yeah. Just a little sleep deprived."

"You didn't work through the night, I hope."

"No."

"Are you staying at your place now?"

She nodded.

"Well, if that's affecting your sleep, it's understandable, in light of what happened there."

She knew he was trying to be helpful, but she was still annoyed. "Nothing happened there. Middleton was long gone when I got home."

"I didn't mean to upset you," Jack said.

"I'm not upset. I'm just stating a fact. I've dealt with much worse."

He was silent for a moment. "So being there doesn't make you anxious?"

"No," she lied.

"Good."

The server brought the menus, and they ordered drinks.

"If it did," Jack said, "I was going to say the cause might not be the break-in directly but something you associate with it—maybe something that happened years ago."

Now she was more than annoyed. In fact, she was seriously pissed. She hadn't given him permission to psychoanalyze her, and it was presumptuous of him to try. Even counting whatever Sally had told him when she was asleep, he knew almost nothing about her.

"I'm sorry," she said, "but I'm not very good company tonight. I think I should go."

He looked stricken. "Please, I didn't—"

"Another time," she forced herself to say.

Over his protests she put down some money for the drink and left. Her anger so masked her dread that during the drive home she was conscious of nothing else. But when she got in bed, it was the same story. She would start awake every few minutes, her heart pounding. At three she drove to headquarters and sacked out in the crib.

Jack called her later in the morning.

"Just wanted to see if you were all right," he said.

"I'm fine. I apologize for leaving."

"No, I'm the one who should apologize. I'm glad you're okay."

He rang off without asking her out again. She didn't know whether this signified a temporary or a permanent backing off. Whichever it was, she didn't know how she felt about it.

With their current investigation stalled, she and Rick took on another robbery. Two white males wearing stockings over their heads had forced their way into the home of an elderly woman, tied her up in a chair, and robbed her of cash, jewelry, silverware, and an old TV they'd dropped in the driveway and left there. The intruders had parked their van where the bound victim had a partial view of it through a window. She could see the name "Yolanda" spray-painted on the side in purple, and she remembered the van from a few months ago, when she'd had a new roof put on her house.

Armed with this information, they ID'd the men, both of them former employees of a roofing company, and using a SWAT team arrested them Thursday afternoon at the van owner's garage apartment. The suspects, who were watching "Oprah" and smoking pot, were too stoned to appreciate the gravity of the situation.

"Hey, I know you," the van owner's buddy said to her. "You're that chick on TV."

"Try to think of me as your arresting officer. Who's Yolanda?"

"His girlfriend," the buddy said.

"Ex-girlfriend," the van owner said. "The bitch."

Rick found most of the loot in a closet. They put it in the trunk, and as they drove to the station, Cynthia turned around and looked at the men, who'd gone somber on them.

"You do know you aren't master criminals," she said.

They shrugged.

"No way we wouldn't have caught you. So it's a good thing all you did to that old lady was scare the hell out of her. Know what I'm saying?"

The rest of the day was spent getting statements and doing related paperwork. Rick left around six, but she lingered at her desk, considering whether she should check into a motel. She'd been using the office crib every night for a few hours. It enabled her to do her job, but she wasn't operating at maximum efficiency, and that made her not just a less competent investigator but a potential danger to herself and her partner, and anybody else who might have to depend on her. A solid eight hours at a motel would sharpen her up. She feared, though, that it might also tempt her into abandoning her apartment altogether, and if she did that,

Middleton would have won.

She was saved from a decision, at least temporarily, by the report of a hit and run in North Hill. She volunteered to take it, and when she arrived on the scene, the eleven-year-old victim had already been taken to the hospital. Two uniforms were holding a witness, a man who'd been walking his dog. One of them was Williams, the handsome cop she'd met at the beginning of the Alicia Bradford case. She took him aside.

"How's the boy?" she said.

"Broken arm, a few scrapes. They're gonna check him for internal injuries, but my guess is he'll be okay. What I can tell, he ran out in the street. The car couldn't have been going too fast, or he'd be a lot worse off. I doubt we would've charged the driver."

"Did he see anything?"

"He got hit in the butt. All he saw was the street coming at him."

"What about your witness?"

"Maybe you can do better than me."

"Nobody else saw anything?"

"I took the liberty of knocking on some doors. Didn't find anybody."

"Okay, thanks."

She asked him for the boy's and the man's names and went over to the man. "Hello, Mr. Budlong," she said. "Can you describe the car that hit Danny?"

"As I told the officers, I didn't get a very good look it. I heard this thump and saw Danny flying through the air. It looked like he was jumping; his feet and his hands were out in front of him. But then he hit the street and just laid there, moaning. I hurried over to him and yelled for help. I was worried another car would come along."

"You did all the right things, sir. Did you happen to notice the color of the car?"

"Red, I think. Or maybe brown. It was hard to tell in the street light."

"How about the make?"

"I don't know cars, I'm sorry."

"Small or large?"

"Small, I believe."

"Anything distinctive about it? Broken light, a dent, a bumper sticker?"

He shook his head. "Not that I saw."

"See any numbers or letters on the license plate?"

"No, ma'am."

She gave him her card and let him go. She called the hospital, learned that Danny was still in emergency, and decided to wait until tomorrow to see him.

Williams walked with her to her car.

"Really something, the way you cracked that serial-killer case," he said.

"Thanks."

"I'm Steve, by the way."

"Cynthia."

"Your day about over, Cynthia?"

"Looks like it."

"Mine too. Wanna get a drink? On me, in celebration of your collar."

It was another excuse for putting off her sleeping arrangements. "Sure," she said. "Why not?"

He gave her directions to a bar. She got there ahead of him, and when he showed up, he was wearing dark slacks and a blue dress shirt. He was even better looking in civvies. He was also, she reminded herself, a good decade younger than she was. But they were only having a drink, and anyway Jack must be a decade older. So on average she wasn't a cradle robber.

They got a table against the wall and swapped cop stories over a few beers. He was a good storyteller, funny and self-deprecating. He had Jeff's ease around women, though maybe he was a little less engaged, a little more calculating. But she didn't mind. She enjoyed listening to him, and when her concentration wavered, she enjoyed staring into his brown puppy-dog eyes.

Those eyes were now looking at her questioningly.

"What?" she said.

"I said… Never mind. You okay?"

"Yeah. But it's late. I probably should be going." Where, she still hadn't made up her mind.

"My apartment's not far from here. How about we go there and I fix you a cup of coffee for the road?"

She smiled at him. "They serve coffee here, don't they?"

"You don't want their coffee, believe me. I'm really like five minutes away."

One more delay. "Okay. I'll follow you."

When they arrived, he said, "I'll warn you, it might look like the black hole of Calcutta."

It wasn't quite that bad, but the décor consisted mainly of strewn clothing and beer bottles, which he gathered up and stuck in a lamp-table cabinet.

"You'll forget you did that," she said, "until the next time you do it."

Ignoring this, he opened a kitchen cabinet. "All I've got is mugs. Redskins one okay?"

"Sure."

She went in the kitchen and stood behind him. He filled a mug with tap water, put it in the microwave, and opened a jar of instant coffee.

"This is the better coffee?" she said.

"Much better, by comparison."

She watched him waiting for the water to heat up. He had broad shoulders and no waist to speak of, despite all the beer bottles. His dark hair looked thick and soft.

He took out the mug and spooned in the instant. Turning to her, he said, "You take anything in it?"

She raised a hand and touched his hair. It was all the encouragement he needed. He began kissing and caressing her, rather expertly.

"Let's go in the bedroom," she said.

He showed her the way, and they helped each other out of their clothes.

"Got a condom?" she said.

"Uh-huh."

"Show me."

He took one from the bed-table drawer. She pushed him down on the bed, put it on him, and straddled him for a pleasant but not especially thrilling few minutes. The drinks or lack of sleep made her orgasm seem to be happening at a remove, like distant thunder. She kissed him and climbed off and plummeted into sleep, blissful sleep. In the middle of the night she woke up and found her way to the bathroom, then crawled back in bed. He turned over and put his hand on her breast.

"Hi," he said.

"Hi," she said, gently removing his hand.

"So how come a beautiful woman like you isn't married?"

"What's wrong with me, you mean?"

"No. I—"

"Or is your point that women over a certain age *should* be married?"

He laughed. "I'm not going to get out of this, am I?"

"I'd plead the fifth, if I were you."

"How about I ask you something else?"

"Okay."

"Why'd you become a cop? Not, you know, why you, a woman. Just why you. Your dad in law enforcement?"

Her womanhood did seem to be hiding in the question, but she let it go. "Not that I know of."

"You don't know what he does?"

"He took off before I was born."

"Oh. So was it was just you and your mom?"

She wondered if this was simple curiosity or another run at a repeat. To satisfy her own curiosity she answered him. "We lived with her father in the country. 'Paps' I called him. He was a big man with a bushy beard, and he kept an orange hard hat in his truck. But that's pretty much all I remember about him. He died when I was six."

"Your mom marry again?"

The *again* had to be for her sake. His delicacy surprised her. "She was fifteen when she had me," she said, "and as a single mother she didn't have much opportunity to marry."

"She live around here?"

"She died when I was nine."

"Jeez," he said. "I'm sorry."

He was a nice guy, she thought, even if he put his better qualities in the service of his sexual appetite. But she'd allowed him too many questions. Time to end it.

"Did you go live with relatives?" he said.

"Foster care."

"I hear that can be tough."

"I got moved around a lot, that was the worst of it for me." *Except for being somebody's paycheck, a commodity. The reason she'd run away.* "What about you? You grow up around here?"

"Yeah. Right here, actually, in North Hill."

"What was that like?"

"It was good. I did the usual kid things. Played a lot of sports."

"Had a lot of girlfriends."

"A few. In the summers when I was older, I worked for my dad. He's a plumber. My mom manages the business, and my two brothers work for him full-time now."

"But not you."

"Nope. They don't hold it against me, though. And I help out when I can, if they need an extra hand."

"Sounds like a tight-knit group."

"Yeah. Being a cop, you know, I've seen some pretty messed-up kids. It's made me appreciate what I had growing up."

He was also a more serious guy than she'd given him credit for being. She kissed him on the cheek.

"I have to go," she said.

He got dressed too and walked her to her car.

"Wanna have a real date sometime?" he said. "You know, dinner and a movie or something."

She shook her head. "We already had the something, and it was nice, but you make me feel too old. So thanks, but no thanks."

"We could just have a drink and talk. I like talking to you."

"Yeah, we could do that sometime. You be careful, now."

She opened the door and climbed in.

"A man came into our house," she said, "and raped and murdered my mother." She shut the door on his startled face and drove away. A few miles down the road an explosion of grief shook her and released itself in a long, ragged wail. Fighting to steer, she pulled into a derelict gas station and parked behind it. She held herself tightly, shrieking and rocking, tears and snot dripping down her face. How long this went on she didn't know, but it felt like years, a lifetime. When she drove back onto the road, there was a flush of red behind the spidery trees.

At her apartment she showered and put on her robe and sat on the couch. She'd gotten no more sleep than she would have in the crib, but she didn't feel dragged out. She felt instead a kind of lightness, as if a heavy burden had slipped from her back. And then she understood why. Jack's shrewd guess had been right. Her anxiety had flowed from Middleton's connection to her past: the home-invasion murder of her mother. She hadn't wanted to acknowledge the parallel, obvious as it was, because it would stir old memories.

The first months after her mother's death she'd been too stunned to feel anything much, though she'd believed all sorts of impossible and contradictory things—that her mother was in the hospital and would come for her soon; that this was a test and if she was good, she'd be allowed to go home; that every night while she slept her mother came into the room and watched over her. Eventually the beliefs faded and horrific memories took their place. That was when she discovered her trick of diverting her attention. She did the same thing with nightmares after the fact, which seemed to rob them of their power and frequency. Now she seldom dreamed, or didn't remember her dreams. And as another way of keeping the lid on Pandora's box, or so she'd thought, she'd never told anyone about her mother, not the children she'd lived with, not her teachers, not her work friends, not even Sally. Not until tonight. And she'd let tonight happen because of Jack.

But there was more. She saw it now, amazed at her own obtuseness. The parallels didn't end with Middleton. From the beginning of the Alicia Bradford investigation she'd resisted her awareness of certain similarities between herself and Alicia. Both of them had grown up in rural homes, both had lost their families at a young age, both had found solace in literature. They were even associated with the same college. If it hadn't been for these connections, she doubted that the break-in would have affected her so much. After all, she dealt with crimes and criminals every day, and although they got to her sometimes, they didn't undermine her sanity. This was the life she'd chosen.

She thought back to the two deputies who'd steered her in this direction. Watching them investigate Harley's death, she'd wanted to do what they did. But why? It seemed to her now that the cause must have been her mother's murder, even though she'd worked so hard not to remember it. Was she after a kind of redress, catching the guilty as hadn't been done in her mother's case, and giving the innocent some sense of closure and order restored, as hadn't happened for her? Or was it darker than that? A compulsion to take revenge or to compensate for her helplessness as a child by being the one with power?

Her heart, that dense tangle of feeling and impulse, swallowed up her questions. Maybe the cause had been all of these. But whatever it had been, she believed, or hoped, that the job had acquired less neurotic meanings for her, just as Sally's farm had become more than a memorial to Bobby. Or Jack's boat more than a self-conscious metaphor for happiness: it had given him time with his daughter. Things changed, and in some ways this was a comforting thought.

Indulging her new sense of ease, she put her head back and rested her eyes. Her cell began ringing. She opened her eyes and fumbled for it on the coffee table.

"Yeah?" she said.

"Cyn?" Rick said. "Where are you?"

"I—what time is it?" Strong daylight enflamed the curtains.

"Ten-fucking-a.m. Another beauty shop just got hit."

"Where?"

"Here in town, corner of Sixth and Bromley."

"Okay. I'll meet you there."

Chapter 22

On Friday afternoon the driver in the North Hill hit and run, an eighteen-year-old girl, showed up at the North Hill station with her parents and turned herself in. Steve Williams called Cynthia to give her the word. She was writing her report when Sampson summoned her to his office.

"Close the door," he said when she entered.

He held up a folder. "This is the DNA report on the hair. We've got a match with the first two women who were abducted, and with a woman in Maryland, the unsolved case you'd asked the Frederick police about—they sent us her DNA analysis for comparison. The fourth packet of hair shares DNA with Middleton."

She took this in. "His mother?"

"That's the theory."

"And there's no match to Alicia Bradford?"

He shook his head. "Nothing in Middleton's apartment or car to connect them, either."

"What about the house in Frederick?"

"Maryland techs are dealing with that. And taking their time."

She thought she saw where this was going. He didn't want egg on his face.

"I understand from Bullock," he said, "you were looking at a couple of other individuals."

"Yes, sir. But it was all preliminary. Jeff and I only worked the case for—"

He waved his hand impatiently. "I can keep things under wraps for a few days, and maybe Maryland will have some good news for us by then. But in case they don't, I'll need something to give the press—more evidence implicating Middleton, a new lead, whatever you can come up with. And I mean you alone. Understood?"

She nodded.

"You need anything, ask Bullock. He knows about this."

"Yes, sir."

"He also knows that if it gets out, I'll tear him a new one."

That night she planned out a course of action, beginning with a new search of Middleton's apartment, which she'd learned from Roger was still intact. She drove there on Saturday morning. Taped to the manager's door was a cartoon poster of a ghost floating in front of a bare tree. Halloween was tomorrow, she remembered. The manager, an elderly man with bushy eyebrows, said as he handed over Middleton's key, "You're the one who found him, aren't you? The one on TV?"

"Yes, sir."

"I thought so. That man who killed him, he deserves a medal."

"He broke the law too."

"Law or no law, I don't see how killing a devil could be bad."

She climbed the stairs and let herself in. She concentrated on areas where the previous search may have been less than thorough. In the kitchen she pulled out pots and pans and lifted plates and bowls. She moved on to the bathroom and unfolded the towels and washcloths. She went through the pockets of the shirts and coats in his closet, releasing a faint human scent: Middleton's lingering presence.

When she finished with the closet, she stared at the photograph of his pretty, coldly smiling mother. A more memorable face than his, a stronger ghost haunting this place. Middleton was memorable only for his deeds. She felt again the vast disproportion between his stunted humanity and the suffering he'd created.

She said to the silence, not expecting an answer, "Did you kill Alicia?"

From her car she called the Hagerstown prison and set up an interview with Fallon for that afternoon. Driving there, she saw that autumn was past its peak. The trees along the highway raised naked arms to the overcast sky, and dead leaves swirled on the pavement. The day suited her mood. Until Sampson had called her in, she'd tried not to think about

Fallon. She'd liked him, and sympathized with him, and then he'd shrunk himself to Middleton's size. She didn't want to know what he'd become.

He was a different man. That much was clear as soon as she saw him. He was greasy-haired, stubbled, softer-looking. His dark eyes had a dull stare. It was as if he'd never sobered up from the liquor he'd drunk at Middleton's. He seemed utterly becalmed, without purpose or hope, like a spirit she'd raised from the underworld. The only lively thing about him was the orange of his prison jumpsuit.

She'd asked that he not be restrained, and when he sat down across from her, he rested his big hands on the table.

"How are you, Mike?" she said.

He gave a slight shrug. "I heard you found his trophies. That was good work."

"Thanks. It's why I came to see you, actually."

"Yeah?"

"We got the DNA test results from all the hair. No match to Alicia."

This revived him a bit. "Decker was here a few days ago. So I know the Maryland cops didn't find any bodies. You got anything else?"

"Not on our end. But Maryland forensics isn't done yet; they could still come up with something."

He nodded. A flicker in his eyes, however, suggested he'd thought of the other possibility.

"I need to know," she said, "exactly what Middleton told you about Alicia."

"Just what I told Decker. He brought her there, to his house. He raped and tortured her, and then he strangled her."

"And dumped her body where they couldn't find any bodies."

"He confessed. What more do you need?"

"Unless forensics can link the two of them, more than that."

He started to speak, but an odd expression crossed his face and he shut his mouth.

"What?" she said.

"Nothing. I just remembered something. But it's nothing."

"Mike."

"I asked him to tell me about Alicia, and he said he kidnapped her outside her office. So I said, Don't you mean outside the grocery store, and he said, Yeah, he forgot."

"So maybe the CPA was his last victim."

"But why would he say he killed her?"

"You know why."

He looked down at his hands. "I know he did it. But suppose he didn't. He was still a murderer. The hair proves it."

Her first impulse was to say nothing. He was shielding himself from his own monstrousness—made all the more monstrous, she believed, because he'd used Middleton as a scapegoat for his embittered discontent. Without the justification of an uncle's vengeance, punishing a murderer would be his final defense. *Let him hold onto it*, she thought. It might help him endure prison. But she wanted more for him than that. She wanted him to live.

"You didn't kill him because he murdered those other women," she said. "You killed him because of Alicia."

If this struck home, it didn't show. She left him sitting there stone-faced.

On the way back, she stopped at the Frederick police station and found Decker at his desk.

"Just couldn't stay away, could you?" he said.

"Not as long as your evidence tests aren't done."

"Well, you might have a long wait. The state lab is way behind. Besides which, we caught our man red-handed, and I do mean red-handed, thanks to you. And your guys solved my old murder case. So we're already happy. Now buy me some pie and coffee and tell me why those tests are so important."

She drove them to the hole-in-the-wall of his choice and filled him in.

"Boss man put you in charge, huh?" he said.

"For a few days."

"He's not as dumb as I thought. But I'd still bet on Middleton. I'd say he pretty much filled the quota of serial killers for these parts. And we know he changed his M.O. to get to you. Maybe he moved on from collecting hair, too."

This made sense, but somehow she couldn't rest in it. On the drive home she kept thinking about Walter and Freddy, and when she reached the town limits, she decided to head west to North Hill and have a talk with Freddy. She didn't necessarily consider him a suspect. It was more that she wanted to eliminate him. But this time she'd really grill him.

She'd get him to talk about his relationship with his sex-offender boarder and his mother. She'd stir up whatever ugliness lurked beneath his eerie composure and try to judge whether it could have bred a murderer.

A party was in progress at his house, a Halloween party. Crudely carved jack-o-lanterns lighted the porch steps, and college-age kids in face paint and eye masks stood on the porch drinking beer. The heavy base beat of the music coming from inside drowned out their voices. She didn't see how Freddy could stand it.

She made her way through the porch crowd into an ocean of throbbing sound and walked down the hall to Freddy's. Someone in a skeleton mask and suit stood in his doorway.

"Freddy?" she said.

The skeleton shook its head.

"Move aside, please."

She went past it into a roomful of costumed partygoers. The junk on Freddy's table had been cleared, or rather heaped under it, and in its place was a circle of lighted candles. The circle held other circles: a ring of mammy and uncle salt and pepper shakers, a smaller ring of black babies in the mouths of alligators, a still smaller one of boys eating watermelon slices. In the center was a little bust of a smiling red-lipped black man with a single arm palm up. A bank, she guessed, that delivered coins via the hand to the mouth. She also guessed that Freddy wouldn't have made a mockery of his mother's racist collectibles.

"Where's Freddy?" she said to a girl in a bright red wig and devil horns.

"Freddy's gone."

"Gone where?"

"I mean he died. He had another heart attack last night. He must've called for an ambulance, but by the time they got here, it was too late. You're that cop lady from the other day, aren't you?"

"Yeah."

"Nobody's said if we'll get kicked out or what. That's why we're having the party tonight. What do you think?"

"I think you shouldn't be in here." Cynthia held up her badge and shouted over the din, "Sheriff's office! Everybody out. This room is private property."

"But the beer's in the refrigerator," someone said.

"Take it with you," Cynthia said.

After they'd filed out lugging cases and six-packs, she snuffed the candles with her fingertips and shut the door behind her. Futile gestures, she knew. They'd return as soon as she left.

Chapter 23

She met Jimmy Smoot for breakfast at a diner near headquarters. Jimmy was of her retired partner's generation, but respectful of women cops and polite to just about everybody. He was an oddity in his profession, a Southern gentleman. In the summer he wore a seersucker suit and a panama hat with a feather; in the winter, a heavier suit and a felt hat with a feather. He was slight man with a prominent, reddish nose that had given him, inevitably, the nickname Snoot, which he accepted in his gentlemanly way. He was also a methodical and thorough investigator who forgot nothing.

"I want to tell you something," she said, "but you need to keep it under wraps for a few days."

His mild blue eyes studied her face. "Yes, ma'am."

"I saw in Alicia Bradford's case file that you interviewed her aunt and uncle."

He nodded.

She told him about the DNA tests. "Anything you learned from that interview," she said, "I'd like to know."

"I don't have my notes with me."

"But you remember it all anyway."

"More or less," he said with a little smile. "Miss Bradford graduated from Princeton and went on to Yale, where she had a boyfriend—her aunt remembered his name because he was the only one, far as she knew. He didn't last too long, the aunt didn't know why. I checked him out.

He's been in Paris, France, since August, doing research on some French writer." Jimmy cast his eyes toward the ceiling. "Sort of rhymes with Tex Ritter. Derrida, I believe it is. Anyway, after Miss Bradford got her Ph.D. from Yale, she taught at the University of Chicago for three years. I talked to some people in her department there. No boyfriends that anybody remembers. No trouble that anybody remembers."

"Why'd she leave after only three years? Was it a temporary position?"

"A lady I spoke with said it was her choice. They were surprised, in fact. Mary Weaver's kind of a step down from the University of Chicago."

"She didn't give them a reason?"

Jimmy Smoot shook his head and took a bite of scrambled egg.

Dead end. But since they were still eating, she said, "The Bradfords tell you anything about her childhood?"

"I didn't ask about that."

"Right."

"But it came up a couple times, around the edges. Mr. Bradford is a lawyer who joined his father's firm, which his grandfather started. His brother, on the other hand, dropped out of college and traveled around, painting pictures. So I think Mr. Bradford saw his brother as a..."

"Black sheep?"

"I was going to say *queer duck*, but I guess we don't say that anymore."

"You can say anything you want to me, Jimmy."

"He—Mr. Bradford—also considered his brother to be irresponsible. He said his mother would send the brother money to keep his family from starving."

"I wonder if Alicia picked up on any of that," Cynthia said.

"Children generally do," Jimmy Smoot said.

When she asked for the check, Jimmy had already come to an understanding with the waitress, and there was nothing to be done but thank him. Courtliness was hard to crack. She went to headquarters and spent the day with Alicia's things in police possession. She examined her phone records, looking especially for Walter Lewis's number. Nothing. It was strange that Alicia had put his home number on her cell but had never called him, not that she'd needed to with their offices so close. Or would want to, if she were his lover—unless she'd ceased to care about being circumspect. This fitted Cynthia's initial idea of a motive for Walter wanting to murder Alicia, but now she wasn't so sure he'd kill to preserve his marriage.

She looked at the laptop's files, emails, and search history, but found nothing of significance in them, either. Alicia had saved a copy of Frost's "Directive," and Cynthia opened it and re-read it. Obviously, the poem had made an impression on her, just as it had on Cynthia, and maybe for the same reasons, but that observation didn't lead anywhere. She went through everything again, on the off chance she'd missed something, but nothing new jumped out at her. All that was left was talking to Walter. She would have to get him to expose himself, as she'd intended to do to Freddy, but her history with him wouldn't make that easy.

Driving home, she decided to drop by Mrs. White's and get Jeff's advice.

"Come on in, honey," Mrs. White said. "You're just in time for supper. We eating a little bit early, on account of the trick a treaters."

"Oh, no, I couldn't."

Mrs. White took Cynthia's arm and pulled her inside. It was her day, it seemed, for running up against the obstinacy of good will. Mrs. White guided her into a little dining room where Jeff and Denise Johnson were sitting at the table.

"It's the literary detective," Jeff said.

"Come to see her gimpy sidekick," she said.

"Go, girl," Denise said.

A pair of metal crutches was propped against the wall, and gesturing at them Cynthia said, "I see you've graduated."

"Yep. I'm starting desk duty next week."

"Great."

"I don't know how ya'll have managed without me."

"Mr. Modest," Denise said.

"It hasn't been easy," Cynthia said. "Roger bemoans your absence every day."

Jeff grinned. "Soon he'll get to bemoan my presence."

The food was already on the table: big bowls of greens, snap beans and mashed potatoes, platters heaped with cornbread and fried chicken. She hadn't realized she was hungry until she began eating, and when she'd cleaned her plate, Mrs. White insisted on her taking another piece of chicken. "That tall frame of yours could use some filling out," she said.

"Never mind your arteries," Jeff said.

"You already had seconds," his mother said to him.

"I know. I'm an addict. I need a twelve-step program."

"You could start by apologizing to chickens," Denise said.

This tickled Mrs. White so much she choked on her iced tea.

At the end of the meal Mrs. White and Denise took the dishes into the kitchen, and she and Jeff talked. Having brought him up to date, she said, "It's going to be tricky with Walter. The last time I spoke to him, he hung up on me."

Jeff thought for a moment. "He won't feel like a suspect, with Middleton all over the news. Maybe you could set it up as a friendly conversation—somewhere else than at headquarters."

"Even that could be difficult."

"Well, you'll need a good lie to get him anywhere."

"Right."

"And I know it goes against the grain, but you might say you're sorry for being such a hard ass."

"Okay. I could do that. And maybe I could capitalize on the fact that I held off asking his wife about his relationship with Alicia, or his Sunday evening drive, which would've amounted to the same thing. I could say it was out of consideration for him."

"The guile of the serpent," Jeff said. "You might be working for the wrong team. But suppose you do reel him in. How you gonna ask *the* question?"

"Who was it he didn't call at Gilley's?"

"That's the one."

"Don't know. Maybe if I met him at Gilley's, I could work something out."

Mrs. White and Denise returned bearing dessert plates laden with slabs of chocolate cake.

"We better eat up," Denise said. "Kids'll be coming soon."

They scarfed the cake down, and Jeff got up and hobbled on his crutches to the front door. Denise brought him a chair and handed him a big bowl of candy.

"Where's my mask?" he said.

"I'll ask your momma," Denise said.

She came back with a rubber mask. Jeff pulled it over his head and turned to Cynthia.

"Pretty scary, huh?" he said.

"I never thought of Bill Clinton as particularly scary," she said.

"Oh, they won't know who Clinton is. They'll just see a white man— scariest thing of all in this neighborhood."

She left before the first trick-or-treaters rang the bell, driving slowly past the little groups of ghosts and superheroes walking along the road, most with an adult in tow. She stopped at a drugstore near her apartment and bought a medium-sized bag of candy, which she thought would be enough for the few children she'd seen around her complex. Over the next hour and a half her doorbell rang three times. The last was right at eight, so she gave the almost full bag to the solitary Leather Mask on her doorstep.

"Cool," he said.

From his size and voice, she put him at around ten. "You been doing this by yourself?" she said.

"No, I was with some other kids in their neighborhood."

"Where do you live?"

"Over there." He pointed across the way, in the vicinity of Mrs. Morelli's.

"You know trick or treating's over, right?"

"Yeah."

"Okay. I'll keep an eye on you until you're home. And don't forget to brush your teeth."

She watched him walk across the commons and go into his apartment. Then she switched off her outside light, went to her computer, and Googled Walter Lewis. There wasn't a lot. A brief biography said he was born in Texas but grew up in various places around the country and in Europe, the only child of an Army officer. He'd gotten his undergrad degree from USC, where he was also on the wrestling team, and an M.F.A. from the University of Iowa. Was the wrestling, she wondered, a way to show his military dad he wasn't a queer duck? Whether it had that significance, he would have known how to wrestle Alicia into his car.

After grad school he'd been writer-in-residence at several colleges in the west. He'd been on the move, then, since childhood. No real roots anywhere. His poems had appeared in a number of magazines with "Review" in the title, and he had two books of poetry to his credit. As for the poems themselves, she could locate only six of them. Five had the same title—"Landscape Variations"—followed by non-sequential numbers, the highest being twenty-six; so there were at least that many of them. They were all fairly brief nature descriptions that stressed the transient beauty of things—shifting sunlight, dissolving clouds, rain patterns, the effects of wind on trees and water. One of them began:

High in the pines the last
rose-colored light
milder than grace
more silent than peace
gathers itself for flight
into the past.

She didn't like Walter Lewis, her suspicions aside, and she didn't want to like these poems. To some extent she succeeded. They were subtly egocentric. It wasn't just that he was the only human being in them, the usual thing in lyric poetry. It was that he seemed to address himself alone. He was like a talker whose only subject is himself, and who doesn't care who's listening, so long as he has an audience. Although in Walter's case, you wondered how important the audience was. But she had to admit that the poems possessed a sort of quiet yearning that touched something in her. Intentionally or no, he'd held the mirror up to nature. He'd done what artists do.

The sixth poem was much longer and appeared at first to be less self-involved. She assumed it was about his wife and—given the date—their firstborn. Hidden in outer darkness, the unidentified speaker watched a woman and a child on the other side of a glass door dancing together, the boy's feet on the woman's feet, the woman moving her lips in silent song as she leaned down to hold the tiny hands. This tender scene, rendered somewhat creepy by the observer's detachment, led to a meditation on how words not only fail to capture reality but go on to supplant it, like an imposter assuming someone else's identity. She picked up allusions to Shakespeare and Wallace Stevens, and she had the sense of other references, all of them contributing to a philosophical discourse that ended with a bleak comment on the original image:

There and not there
no one here
mute ghost in the night.

She came away feeling a little sorry for Walter in spite of herself, and more sorry for his wife and children.

Chapter 24

The next morning she called Laura, the English department secretary, to find out whether Walter had office hours after his three o'clock poetry-writing class. He didn't, but Laura said he generally stayed past five, when she left. Putting off going home to the family, Cynthia thought.

She rang him at 4:40.

"Mr. Lewis," she said, "this is Cynthia Westbrook, of the sheriff's office."

"Yes, I remember," he said dryly.

"I'm glad I reached you. I wanted to apologize."

"Apologize?"

"Yes. The purpose of an interrogation is to shake things out of people. Unfortunately, they aren't always the right people. But with you I did try to take that possibility into account. When I interviewed your wife, I didn't ask her about your friendship with Alicia, or your Sunday evening drive."

After a moment, he said, "I see."

"And when I called you a couple of weeks ago, I was trying to get a strong reaction, so I could gauge whether you might have broken into my apartment. It was how I eliminated you as a suspect."

"But you thought I could have done it."

"I don't know you, Mr. Lewis. That's where I have to begin."

Another pause. "Okay. I'm grateful, of course, that you found the man."

She took a silent breath. "There's been a development concerning him, which is another reason I called. I can't discuss it over the phone, but I'd like to tell you about it. I'm hoping you might be able to help us. Are you going home soon?"

He hesitated. "Yes."

"Could you meet me at Gilley's? It's on your way, or one of your ways, and I'm not far from there."

"All right."

"Thanks. I won't keep you long."

There were half a dozen customers in Gilley's, all dressed in work clothes and ball caps. When she went up to the bar, one of them patted the empty stool beside him and said, "Have a seat, pretty lady, and let ole Bob buy you a drink."

"No, thanks, Bob," she said.

Rhonda, standing behind the bar, said, "Hon, you don't want to mess with her. She's the po-lice."

"Zat right?" Bob said.

"Yep."

"Well, you can arrest me any time, darling."

"I may just do that, Bob, depending on what shape you're in when you leave."

In the silence this produced, she asked for a beer and carried it to the booth nearest the wall phone. She chose the side facing away from the phone so Walter would have it in his field of vision. With her fingers around the cold bottle, she went over her plan. If he'd killed Alicia on Sunday, it was possible that something in their Friday afternoon conversation had set him off. She'd focus on that conversation. But she couldn't do it directly; she'd need her lies, such as they were. The most important thing was to recognize opportunities and exploit them.

When Walter Lewis came in, she smiled and waved him over. He sat down across from her, looking first at the phone and then at her, his lips compressed.

She lifted her bottle of beer. "Off duty," she said. "Would you like a drink? It's on me."

"No, thanks."

Taking a small sip, she decided to go slow with him. "I saw that the college held a memorial service."

"Yes."

"Did you speak at it?"

"I read a poem."

"What was the poem?"

"Something of mine Alicia had liked in particular. A description of trees."

She wondered if it was the one about light leaving the pines, but to ask him didn't seem wise. It might make him suspicious of her.

"That must have been difficult," she said.

"Yes."

"Why was it one of her favorites, did she say?"

"No. She just said she liked it. But I think now it may have had to do with her family. I didn't know about them until I saw her uncle, the one who wasn't arrested, on the news."

This was consistent with what he'd said about the non-personal nature of his and Alicia's conversations, which didn't mean it was the truth. "Is it a poem about loss?" she said.

He nodded. "Not the same kind of loss, but yes."

"Could you tell me about it?"

"It's part of a group of poems. My father was in the Army, and we lived in Germany for two years beginning when I was twelve. I was keeping a journal at the time. It was an early language experiment—I hadn't really thought about being a poet yet. When I re-read it years later, I was struck by the many natural descriptions, not just the trees and lakes and so on but the weather, the clouds, the slant of light, as Emily Dickinson would say. So I decided to take these pieces and use them as jumping off points for a sort of meditation on… time's passage."

The tension had left his face as he talked, and she could see the boy he'd been, the rootless boy who'd anchored himself in the world of words, just as she'd done.

"Interesting," she said. "Sure you won't have a drink?"

"Okay. Maybe a beer."

She signaled to Rhonda, who came and took his order.

"The development I mentioned," she said, "hasn't been made public yet. So if I tell you about it, you'll have to keep it to yourself for a while."

"All right."

She waited until Rhonda had plunked down a beer bottle in front of him. "Our forensic evidence ties Middleton, the dead suspect, to the other women, but not to Alicia."

"I don't understand."

"We haven't entirely ruled him out. Maryland is still doing evidence tests. But we have our eye on someone we'd identified earlier as a person of interest. He lives near the college, and he was in the grocery store the same night Alicia was. We've got him on surveillance tape exiting right after she did."

"But... didn't she disappear like the other women?"

She saw only puzzlement on his face, no hint of relief or self-congratulation at not being a suspect himself. "Not exactly, no. There're some significant differences between her crime scene and the others I can't go into. We also believe she might have known the man in the videotape, casually at least. I told you she bought a gun. We think he could be the reason." She gave him a moment to absorb her several lies. "The first time I asked you to come in for questioning, I said you might know something without realizing it. But I didn't give either of us a chance to find out whether you did. I wonder if we could go through your Friday conversation with Alicia. It might have been her last one with anybody. Maybe she said something that points to the man in the grocery."

"I don't remember anything like that."

"It could be something that seemed trivial at the time. Are you willing to try?"

"Yes, if you think it could help."

"Good. Let's just review everything and see what we have. You said she asked you about a poem—who was it by, again?" She wanted him to feel that he was only supplying information.

"Robert Frost."

"Frost, right. And the title?"

"It's called 'Directive.'"

Since her goal was to keep him talking about Friday afternoon, she said the next thing that occurred to her. "And what did you say to her about it?"

"Basically, that I agreed with the poet and critic Randall Jarrell, who said it was an easy poem to love, but a difficult one to understand."

"Did *she* have an opinion of it?"

He seemed to search his memory. "She said that Frost—Frost in the poem—was like a sorcerer casting a spell."

With a prickling sensation at the base of her neck, she thought of Alicia in her mother's drawing dressed as a sorcerer. "And she didn't say anything about her childhood?"

"No."

"Nothing personal at all?"

"No. Only that she'd enjoyed meeting my family." His Adam's apple moved.

Why the uneasy reaction? He hadn't mentioned this comment before, but it seemed inconsequential, the kind of thing anyone might forget. Then she remembered his wife saying that she'd seen Alicia only once, at the dinner party. If that were true, why would Alicia have brought up his family a month after meeting them?

"Met them where," she said, "at your party in September?"

"Yes."

"But she hadn't been talking about them?"

"No. She just… said it."

His eyes went to the phone again, as if pulled there by some force, and now she was certain there was more.

"It surprised you," she said.

"Yes."

He looked at her again, with an expression she'd seen before. He was a man who had something to get off his chest.

"Why do you think she said it?" she asked.

"I'm not sure. Her voice…" He kept looking at her.

"Something in her voice?" she said encouragingly.

"It's difficult to explain. When we talked, her tone would take on a warmth that didn't seem to come from what she was saying. It was like hearing two things at once, two languages."

She waited now, showing only a confessor's dispassionate interest.

"I first noticed it after the dinner party, and then she stopped doing it for a while, a few days before she…. But when she came to my office on Friday, the warmth was back in her voice."

"Why did she stop?"

"Stop?" He seemed unaware that he'd told her so much.

"Using that tone."

"Oh." He looked away. "I don't know."

A transparent lie. He must have done something to cause her to stop. Had he interpreted her tone as an invitation to an affair, and scared her off by declaring his feelings? Even if she was in love with him, she was a solitary person. He might have come on too strong. It was a theory that fit what Cynthia knew, if he'd told her the truth so far. When Alicia showed up at his office speaking in that warm, intimate way again, he must have wondered whether she was giving him another chance. He'd brooded about it all weekend, and on Sunday evening he'd used his noisy children as an excuse to drive to North Hill and see her, maybe intending to call her first from his office. But then what? Whatever it was, it had led to him standing in front of the phone at Gilley's.

To test her theory, she said, "Do you think she was love with you?"

The question pushed him back in his seat. "I don't know. I don't know. The last thing she said to me was about my family."

The *last* thing. Maybe he'd worried that her conscience would be an obstacle. And if it truly had been the last thing, then they hadn't talked on Sunday. He'd started home without contacting her and stopped at Gilley's, where he'd tormented himself one final time.

She risked an interrogator's directness. "You didn't talk to her on Sunday?"

"No. I thought about it. If I had..."

"Then you'd know," she finished for him.

He looked at her forlornly. "And she might be alive."

She might have been with him, he must mean, instead of at the shopping center. They might be lovers.

"I should go," he said.

They were far beyond the pretense now of talking about the man in the grocery, so she didn't bring him up. "Okay," she said. "Thanks."

He slid out of the booth. "I hope you catch the man, if he is the man."

She sat mulling over their conversation. She'd wrangled a confession from a suspect who didn't know he was one, which argued for its sincerity. But all it convicted him of was desire and regret. She thought of his poems—the sense in them of things slipping away, the feeling that intimacy was elusive. Maybe they were the ultimate explanation of his reluctance to make another attempt at an affair. Or something more than an affair: Alicia was not only pretty and unencumbered by children; she shared his devotion to literature, his feeling of slippage.

It struck Cynthia that the story she'd gleaned from Walter was all from his perspective. She hadn't tried to see it through Alicia's eyes, a lapse she blamed on dodging her identification with Alicia. But at first glance, Alicia's story seemed to mirror Walter's. Attraction and hesitation on her part too. Having lost her family, she might have balked at jeopardizing the happiness of his children, whom she'd played with at the party. But how to explain the gun? It didn't seem to have anything to do with anything. Alicia had bought it, presumably, to defend herself against a serial killer she'd just met without realizing it. And whether Middleton had targeted her as a result of that meeting, he'd apparently chosen Cynthia because she'd questioned him about it. Happenstance and coincidence. They drifted through her thoughts like dense patches of fog.

"'Nother one, hon?" Rhonda said.

"No, thanks."

She got up and put some money on the table. Bob and the others studiously avoided looking at her as she walked to the door. Outside, the night air was crisp and cold. A few stars glittered in the sky, and gazing at them, she wondered what she should do now. With Sampson's help she might be able to get a search warrant for Freddy's, but her gut told her it would be a waste of time.

She climbed in her car and headed home by way of North Hill. It was a less direct route than backtracking through Calvary, but it added only a few miles to the trip. She watched the familiar landscape glide past, the dark fields alternating with bare trees, the saddlery with the white horse on top, the rows of new green tractors at the John Deere dealership. Her territory, her responsibility.

When she came to North Hill, she took the road that led to Greenwood Shopping Center and pulled into the lot. She parked close to where Alicia's car had been found, turned off her engine, and sat. What she was doing here, she had no idea; but she wasn't ready to go home yet. Her mind began playing over the events of the last two days. She thought of Freddy's mocking Halloween wake, and of Fallon, more a dead man walking than anyone on death row. She thought again of the mother's drawing and Frost's poem and wondered whether Alicia had connected them. Both had to do with childhood, lost childhood, like Walter's landscape poems, but Cynthia couldn't get any further than that. Too much fog.

A movement in the rear view mirror caught her eye. She turned her head and saw a short, kerchiefed woman with a shopping bag hurrying toward the bus stop. She glanced at her watch: 7:44. The last bus to Calvary should be arriving soon. The time on Alicia's receipt, she remembered, was 7:41. Walter's words, *the last thing*, floated into her mind, and suddenly a new story formed itself.

What if the Lewis family had reminded Alicia of her own? Young children, the parents both artists as her parents had been, and youthful like them. They even lived in a sort of rural setting. Rough similarities, but perhaps close enough for someone who'd left a prestigious university for a small college in order to be near her childhood home—which she'd needed to see so desperately that she'd failed to check first whether it still existed. That loss might help explain her attraction to the Lewises; they'd filled the vacuum. She must have noticed the "For Sale" sign for the cypress-hidden house on the day of the party, and as her attraction turned into an obsession, she must have imagined living close to them, dropping in on them, becoming a sort of honorary member of the family. Which might also account for their home number in her cell; it was an aspect of her fantasy.

At some point she must have driven out to the house and, blinded by her longing, decided to buy it. Her emotions, meanwhile, would have seeped into her conversations with Walter, whose confusion now made more sense. He wasn't the lover in her fantasy; he was the father. He might have become something more than that, a poet whose work voiced her deepest feelings, and who perhaps led her to read Frost and discover "Directive." But at bottom he must have remained the father, and when he acted like a lover, he destroyed her dream. She withdrew into herself, a change he also misinterpreted. And there the story should have ended. But it hadn't. She'd bought a gun, she'd talked to Walter again in the old, emotion-freighted way, and she'd ended the conversation by referring to his family.

She was saying goodbye to all of them.

From the corner of her eye Cynthia saw the bus pulling in. She jumped out of her car and ran toward it. The woman with the shopping bag was last in line to get on, and Cynthia, striding full out, managed to fall in behind her before the doors closed.

Chapter 25

She fed two dollars into the box and moved down the aisle. A few people glanced at her, but without much interest. Maybe they assumed she was part of the trailer crowd north of Calvary, which old Ms. Dobbins had said was always changing. This could be a reason the passengers on the evening of October 10 hadn't paid enough attention to a blonde stranger with glasses to recognize her later as the woman in the news photos. But the main reason, and the one the stranger would have counted on, was that a woman kidnapped from a parking lot couldn't have been riding a bus at the same time.

Ms. Dobbins was a remarkable witness both for her observational powers and her disregard of logic. To fool everybody else, Alicia had only needed a slight alteration in appearance. She could have cut and dyed her hair, hiding the change under the knit cap she'd worn in the grocery, or pinned her hair up under the cap and slipped on a blonde wig in her car. She could have changed coats there too. In the mother's drawing, Cynthia remembered, she was wearing glasses. She must have switched to contacts at some point, but she could still have used glasses at home, or bought a new pair as a prop. Her Halloween disguise.

The pristine green tractors went past Cynthia's window, followed by the white horse on the store roof. They'd been there when she was a student, and seeing them again from a bus gave her an odd feeling of going backward in time. She almost expected Bill to be waiting for her in his ancient shiny red Lincoln. He would take her home, neither of them saying much, but the silence easy between them, and when they arrived, they'd eat the dinner that he'd prepared. He'd been a good

Southern cook with a partiality to mustard greens. She'd come to love them as much as he did, and she'd also picked up his habit of sopping her cornbread in what he called the *pot liquor* of the greens. She'd been thinking about him, she realized, not just because the anniversary of his death was approaching, but because Alicia Bradford had stirred up long suppressed feelings. Grieving for Bill had been a way of grieving for her mother.

Lost in these reflections, she was surprised when the bus pulled up at the last stop. She watched the other passengers rise and move toward the doors. The sensible thing for her to do would be to stay put. She could ride the bus back to North Hill and return in her car, tonight if she wanted. But instead of heeding her own advice, she got up and descended into Calvary too.

She trailed the little group of fifteen or twenty through the two-block downtown where half the stores were empty, their display windows covered over with newspaper, and the other half closed except for the Hispanic grocery that sold Twinkies. The travelers split at a cross street, plodding toward shabby boarding houses and apartments, and she went on alone. She passed Ms. Dobbins's empty red rocker on the small porch; the old lady's ornery cat must be in for the night. She passed two more houses and a weedy concrete lot, and then she walked through the light of the final street lamp into the darkness.

Shacks and trailers occupied the cleared land on the right side of the road, with the forest preserve rising darkly behind their gold-filled windows. On the left side, a more or less continuous line of trees masked fenced fields and distant farmhouses. She kept inside the tree line and relied on the stars and the piece of moon for illumination, as Alicia would have done. Every now and then, a yard dog across the way would catch her scent and bark, but the shacks and trailers petered out after a couple of miles, and all she had to worry about was being spotted by the sparse road traffic.

She remembered walking another dark and even less traveled road with her mother. On school days the bus would drop her off at the downtown diner where her mother was a waitress, and she'd do her homework in one of the booths sipping a glass of soda through a straw. After business picked up, she'd move to a counter stool at the end and eat the supper her mother brought her. Then she'd read a library book and steal glances at the customers, most of them regulars—shop keepers, laborers, doddery old men. Some of them were nice; they'd chat with her mother and leave a big tip. And some were fake nice; they'd touch her mother when she served them and follow her slender figure with their eyes. Around eleven she and her mother would get in Paps's old pickup and drive the seven miles home, keeping an eye out for deer.

But one winter's night the truck broke down midway and they were forced to walk. To distract Cynthia from the cold and the dark, her mother started them singing *The Twelve Days of Christmas*, and somewhere after the five golden swans, they forgot the words and began to make up things, silly things, that had them both sending up shrieks of laughter into the night. Her mother, she saw now, wasn't just being a good parent; she was also re-living the childhood she'd left too soon. When they reached the house, Cynthia wanted to keep on singing, but her mother, tucking her in, said, "You close your eyes, and you'll be in dreamland before you know it." And so she had been.

Humming *Twelve Days*, she moved along at a careful but brisk pace. Every few minutes she checked her watch with her pocket flashlight, and an hour into her walk she began looking for the realtor's sign on the other side. She finally spotted its black shape and crossed over and followed the gravel tracks that led around the row of cypresses. In the dimness the ruinous house looked vaguely like a head. The leaning posts resembled crooked teeth, the vines along the front a dark, ragged mustache, and the roof a battered hat pulled down over the eyes. She mounted the porch steps and shone her light on the height marks on the inner posts. Alicia must have seen these too and felt, as she did, the ghostly presence of children.

She reached inside a broken window, pushed the sash up, and climbed through. Pieces of glass crunched under the rubber soles of her shoes. There was a fetid odor, but not the distinctive smell of human decomp. She shone her flashlight around the empty room and moved on to the other rooms, inspecting their barren spaces and small closets. All she found were animal droppings, the desiccated bodies of roaches, yellow vines that had made the mistake of growing in through the cracks, and panels of rain-loosened wallpaper drooping floorward like tropical leaves. That left the attic, the entry to which was in the hallway.

She could touch the hatch with her fingertips, but it was still too high. She went to the kitchen and pulled out the cabinet drawers and carried them into the hall. Their bottoms were fiberboard, so she stacked them to get the best use of the hardwood sides. Then she mounted her platform, pushed the hatch aside, and hoisted herself up by her elbows. Her legs dangling into the hallway, she swept her light over the scanty flooring and exposed joists. Nothing here, either, except a bird's nest near one of the vents, with three tiny gray corpses beside it.

She dropped down gingerly and returned to the kitchen. It was at the back of the house, and when she opened the door to the outside, she awakened a memory that she'd had considerable practice in evading. But this time she let it come. *Momma was standing at the sink, her shoulder blades moving like bird's wings above her green tube top. "Just listen to those cicadas," she said. "I didn't know they could be so loud." Cynthia, clearing the table, said, "Why do they do that?" Her mother's shoulders shrugged. "Maybe they just like having a sing-along."*

Cynthia stacked the dishes on the counter and went out and sat on the back steps. Staring into the twilit woods, she listened to the cicadas' rasping song. You could hear distances in it, like you could in a rainstorm. She wondered what the cicadas—funny word, sick-kay-duhs—were singing about. Were they glad to be out of those shells like little suits of armor that she'd seen stuck to twigs? As if to answer her question, a man popped up from behind the gardenia bush beside the house. He had a nice face and light blue eyes. He stared at her like a cat getting ready to spring. Her heart jumped in her throat, and she wanted to cry out, but all she could do was mouth "Momma" as he rushed toward her gripping a piece of firewood.

She went down the back steps, got on her hands and knees, and played her light under the house. Nothing there but acrid-smelling earth. She stood up.

Her head hurt. She touched it, and it was wet. She wobbled up the steps and pushed on the door, but something stopped it. She squeezed half-way through the crack and saw that it was her mother's head, glistening with blood. Her mother lay on her back with her arms and legs sprawled. She was naked except for the tube top bunched around her middle. It was soaked with blood, and blood had pooled beside her. "Momma," Cynthia said. Her mother's eyes stayed fixed on the ceiling. The refrigerator door closed and the man from the bush was there. He was holding a can of beer. "You again," he said.

She walked to the crooked shed and the caved-in chicken house near the forest's edge. Nothing in them, either. She'd been so sure she'd figured it out, and now here she was, miles from anybody and without a car. She could feel the woods towering over her like a black wave about to crash. She turned her flashlight on them and caught something anomalous. Bringing the light back to it, she discovered an upward-pointing arrow carved into one of the tree trunks. She took a closer look. It was about a foot long, and from the brownish color not a recent carving. How had she missed it before? She knew the answer: by escaping the past that was all around her now, as real as the present.

She aimed her light up the tree but saw nothing unusual. Maybe the arrow wasn't pointing up, she thought, but back. She hesitated. Then she stepped into the forest. *Shouts coming from behind her. She was skittering around dark trunks, flying down slopes and over gullies, weightless as in a dream until a branch caught her in the face and snapped her back against the ground. "Hey, little girl!" he was yelling. "You don't want to be in here! There're snakes in here! I bet there're bears and bobcats too!" He sounded like he was coming right to her. She held her breath and screwed her eyes shut. "You had a bad dream, that's all! You fell off the steps and hurt your head! Everything's fine! Your mom wants to see you! She's worried about you!" Then his voice began moving away again, growing angrier as it got fainter. "Show yourself, you little bitch! If I have to find you, you'll wish you were your mother! I'll take my time with you! You hear me, cunt!"*

She walked in what she hoped was a straight line, shining her light back and forth between the leaf-strewn ground and the nearer trees. Not that she had any idea what she was looking for. A gray form moved in the fringe of her beam, and she swung the light in time to see a thin pink tail disappearing into the brush. The 'possum, unlike her, knew where it was. She was the stranger here, the misfit. *Curled in upon herself, sucking her thumb, she heard from every side the cry of the cicadas. It was like an endless shriek, but a shriek with no terror in it, and nothing to do with her, even after it had lodged itself in her breast like some winged creature restlessly fluttering.*

She kept going, and a few minutes later another tail swam into view. No, not a tail, a piece of rope lying across the roots of a tree. She squatted and looked at it. It was tied in a long loop. She couldn't think of any reason for it to be here. She shone her light up the tree and saw in the weak glow of its highest reach a narrow structure with sides and a hatch resting on two branches. About three feet below it was a ladder board.

Where were the other boards? She searched around the tree but didn't find any. She examined the loop again, and a line from Frost's "Directive" popped into her head: *pull in your ladder road behind you.* Could Alicia have done that somehow? Suppose she'd used the rope as a kind of sling, hanging it around a higher rung and sitting in it to pry loose a lower one. A hammer or a small crowbar would have done the job, either of which she could have concealed under her jacket, maybe securing it to herself with the rope. This might also explain the board still in place. If she'd lacked a tether for her sling inside the tree house, she might have lowered the rope to yank the board off and lost her grip.

Lost it, maybe, because she was exhausted. You couldn't hold all those boards while you were climbing; you'd have to take them up one by one. And her exertions would have come after a five-mile hike from the Calvary bus stop. It struck Cynthia that she'd just cast doubt on her theory. Would the scholarly Alicia have had the stamina? Maybe there was a simpler explanation for the missing boards. Someone, the child builders on the verge of moving, perhaps, could have taken the ladder down starting at the top and hauled it away. She could hear Decker saying he'd bet on that. But why would they have left one board up—or just one, if its being out of reach was the reason? And how to explain the rope? They could have used it to bundle the boards, but in that case they wouldn't have discarded it here.

She thought of Laura's description of Alicia in their final meeting. *Serene almost.* The mood of someone free of deep trouble, or who soon will be. If Alicia had resolved to do this, nothing would have stopped her.

Cynthia moved away from the trunk and pointed her light at the tree house again. Its uneven sides made a roof unlikely, and she couldn't see an overhang. She surveyed the nearby trees. Like the tree-house tree, most of them didn't have any limbs closer to the ground than twenty feet. But there was one, a big oak, with a smallish, forked branch about ten feet up. She inspected the trunk above it. Four or five feet higher there was another branch of a similar size, then a middle-sized branch, and above it a number of larger ones ascending in a rough spiral, all fairly close together.

She'd need both hands. She pocketed her light and leaned against the oak, waiting for her eyes to adjust to the darkness. Sounds she hadn't noticed before now invaded her consciousness. She heard rustlings in the undergrowth, the wind's random strumming, the creak and crack of the swaying treetops, and after a few minutes, a melancholy hoo-hoo-hoo. By this point, the forest had emerged in shades of gray. It had a luminescent, dreamlike aura that added to her sense of being adrift in time.

She untied the rope and stretched it out in the leaves. It was about eight feet long. She tied a loop in one end, took off a shoe, and tied other end around the laces. She put her right hand through the loop, stepped under the branch, and tossed the shoe up. It lodged in the fork. She tugged it loose and threw it again. This time it sailed over the branch and dropped in front of her. She untied it, removed her hand from the loop, slipped the other end through, and pulled the rope tight. She put her shoe back on and began to climb, walking her feet up the tree.

It was harder than she'd imagined. The rope burned her hands, and her shoes didn't get much traction. But she managed to throw a leg over one of the forks, and from there to struggle into a sitting position. She considered untying the rope and taking it with her but rejected the idea. Dealing with it would slow her down. She stood up, grabbed the next branch, and wriggled herself onto it. The branch after that presented about the same degree of difficulty, and once she'd perched on it she was able to reach the lowest of the bigger limbs. She was now a good twenty feet off the ground with another twenty or more to go before she could look down at the tree house. Better not to think about it. She concentrated on the placement of her hands and feet, blocking out everything else except the owl's periodic and increasingly louder cries, which began to sound like an ironic commentary on her actions, sadly marking her progress toward nothing. Wait and see, she was telling herself, when a branch broke in her hand. Teetering, she flung herself against the tree, dancing her feet under her, and in the same expanded moment she heard the branch crashing down and sensed more than saw a shadowy counter movement overhead.

Normal time resumed. Her arms were gripping the trunk as if attached to it by suckers. Her heart was thumping against the rough bark. She could feel the abyss beneath her; it was like an open maw waiting to swallow her up. The possibility she'd ignored in her pursuit of Alicia now claimed her attention. If she fell, no one would know where she was. She'd join the ranks of the disappeared, and her car would be found, eerily, near where Alicia's had been parked. Instead of solving a mystery, she would have created a new one.

She twisted her body, keeping her left shoulder against the trunk, and took out her cell. Its bright glow reinforced the absurdity of the situation. The creatures who belonged up here, the owls and the 'possums, didn't carry luminous objects. She checked the power bar. There was some connection, fortunately. She called Jeff.

"Hey," he said. "You talk to Walt?"

"Yep."

"How'd it go?"

"I don't think he did it. But I'm on to something else. You know that house Alicia thought about buying, the one on Mount Zion?"

"Yeah?"

"I'm in the woods behind it. I followed an arrow carved into a tree to a tree house. I think she might have done the same thing."

"I don't get it."

"I think she might have come back to the tree house."

Silence. "You mean you think she's up there?"

"It's a theory."

"Okay. So let me get this straight. You're somewhere in the woods in the dark about to climb up to a tree house."

"There's no ladder."

"Well, good."

"Here's the thing. I took the bus from Greenwood Shopping Center to Calvary and walked here."

"Run that one by me again."

"I was sort of re-tracing her steps, if they were her steps."

"You know how crazy that sounds?"

"Yeah. I do now."

"Well, we can come get you. Momma will have to do the driving."

"Here's the other thing. I'm in a tree near the one with the tree house."

"You're in a tree?"

"Uh-huh."

"Are you fucking nuts?" Then, with his mouth away from the phone: "Not now, Momma."

"I'm almost high enough to take a look," she said. "I'll call you again in a few minutes. But if I don't, you know where I am. Just tell them to go straight back from the arrow. It's carved into a tree near the chicken house."

"Cyn, get outta that tree. You can do this tomorrow with a crew."

"Talk to you later."

She hung up and looked above her. There was a branch to the left of the rotten one. She pulled on it. It felt solid. She grabbed it and continued climbing, and soon was above the tree house, but a clump of dead foliage blocked her view. The next limb up, she saw, would be a stretch—she wished now for the rope—and it might not solve the problem. She'd try something else first.

She shimmied out on her branch to an upright shoot. Holding it with one hand like a saddle horn, she fetched her flashlight and shone it down on the dead leaves. From this angle there was a gap in them that gave her a partial view of the tree house. It had no roof, as she'd thought, and some leaves had fallen into the narrow enclosure. But the soft, surreal beam of the flashlight revealed the upper part of a body lying on its back. A black jacket such as Ms. Dobbins had described was spread out under the head and shoulders. Near the right temple a skeletonized hand still held a snub-nosed revolver, and beneath the hand there was a circular stain, visible on the jacket because it caught the light differently. The elbow of the gun arm touched an inner wall of ladder boards stacked side by side, their nails glinting in the gaps.

She looked at Alicia's face. Decay and insects and maybe larger scavengers like 'possums had reduced it to a few shreds of blackened flesh over bone. A pair of dark-frame glasses lay at an angle beneath the empty eye sockets, and remnants of a blonde wig feathered the jacket like a dingy halo. But a wig wouldn't have disintegrated, she realized. The scalp had sloughed off, or been peeled off. She felt a strong sense of transgression, not her usual reaction to a body. Alicia hadn't wanted to be found; she'd gone to a lot of trouble to disappear forever.

A gust of wind buffeted the branch Cynthia was sitting on. She stuck the flashlight between her teeth and grasped the saddle horn with both hands, remembering for some reason the upward motion she'd glimpsed as she threw herself against the tree. Could it have been the owl taking flight? Now that she thought of it, she hadn't heard him in a while. When the swaying stopped, she gave the corpse a final long look—nothing more to be done for it now—and shimmied backward to the trunk.

She'd intended to start down right away, so as not to keep Jeff in suspense, but Alicia held her there. She knew that her understanding of Alicia, though sufficient to get her here, would never be more than superficial. She'd never know why Alicia had succumbed to her childhood tragedy, any more than she would why others like herself, however damaged, had survived theirs. Maybe it was just a matter of luck, who you happened to meet or didn't meet. Nor would she ever know whether her impression of Alicia's steady downward spiral—the breakup with the boyfriend, the social isolation, the interest in children's literature, the move near the childhood home, the infatuation with the Lewis family—corresponded to reality. It might, but a pattern by its very nature simplified things. Still, she felt compelled to think about the circumstances of the suicide. Alicia could have killed herself in her apartment. Why had she done it here, and why the elaborate ruse to cover her tracks? Cynthia needed a theory at least that could propose answers.

The inception, it seemed, was the visit to the abandoned house. Alicia must have noticed the height marks, as Cynthia had done, and she'd obviously followed the arrow to the tree house. All of this would have resonated with her idealized memory of her family. The marks would have suggested parental love and care; the arrow in plain view, parental indulgence of a child's delights like the tree house. And assuming her familiarity with "Directive," Frost's picture of lost childhood would have intensified her response. This had happened, anyway, by the time she spoke to Walter on Friday, since the poem had been the heart of her farewell.

So the spell had been cast, although it would have been a lesser enchantment than her feeling for the Lewises, which had brought her here. Then sometime between her appointment with Middleton and her phone call to Fallon about a gun, Walter's romantic overtures had ruined her dream, and her thoughts had turned to suicide—but suicide of a special kind, shaped by the house and the poem. *Pull in your ladder road behind you.* In a way, she'd made her own poem out of Frost's, using the house and its surroundings for her materials. Her narrative, following his, was a return to the past and childhood. Her ladder road, the boards nailed to a tree. Her playhouse of make believe, the tree house. Her cracked Grail dispensing salvation, a gun. And through her cold-blooded imitation of the abductions, she'd elevated Frost's rather playful references to secrecy to her main theme, the desire to remain in this lost world forever. She'd constructed her poem well. In a forest preserve her tomb could have stayed aloft for years, and when it fell, its remains mixed with hers might have gone undiscovered beneath the fallen leaves. As it was, she'd been persuasive enough to incite Fallon to murder Middleton and destroy himself.

Cynthia thought of something else, the link she'd felt between Alicia calling Frost in "Directive" a sorcerer and the mother's drawing of Alicia in a sorcerer's costume. She supposed that the comment on Frost had to do with his incantatory beginning, *Back out of all this now too much for us*, and the role he'd assumed of a spiritual guide offering at the end a sort of magical potion. In any case, by making herself disappear Alicia had become a sorcerer in her own poem, and therefore the girl in the drawing. She'd resurrected her childhood self. She'd done this too, it occurred to Cynthia, through the blonde hair and glasses; they hadn't been just a disguise. As in any good poem, things had more than one use.

She wondered about Alicia's final moments. Had she spent them communing with memories of her family, or had the wind and the accidental condolences of an owl disrupted her reverie? Had she squeezed the trigger to seal herself in the past or to shut out the present?

Her cell rang.

"You said a few minutes," Jeff said.

"Not down yet."

"Oh. Are you stuck?"

"No, I'm on my way. I'll call you when I'm on the ground, okay?"

"Careful."

The descent was comparatively fast and easy; her body seemed to like the idea of returning to earth. After she climbed down the rope, she spotted the branch that had almost taken her with it. It lay among the leaves in several large pieces, one of them sticking into the earth like a spear. She contemplated them for a moment, and then she called Jeff back.

"Safe and sound," she said.

"Good. Now that you aren't monkeying around, maybe you can tell me what you saw."

She hesitated, knowing she was about to violate Alicia's wishes, and to heap new misery upon her family.

"Cyn?"

"She's in the tree house. The gun's in her hand."

"Holy shit. How'd you ever figure this one out?"

"Hard to explain. I may have slipped up and relied on woman's intuition."

"Save it for later, then. You still in the woods?"

"Yeah."

"Get outta there. The woods are not your friend. Take it from me."

"Okay. I should call Roger too." But she didn't feel like talking to Roger. To him the case had been a hindrance. He'd be relieved to be rid of it, and that was all. "On second thought," she said, "would you mind calling him? You know where the house is."

"Sure. I like telling Roger where to—"

Overhead, the owl hooted.

"Did I just hear an owl?" Jeff said.

"Uh-huh. I chased him out of the tree when I broke off a branch. But he seems to be back."

"You broke off a branch?"

"It made a lot of noise."

"If a detective falls in the forest, and no one's around to hear her…"

"Yeah, I know. I'll come by tomorrow."

She took out her flashlight and shone it at the upper part of the tree. A pair of brilliant golden eyes stared down at her.

"All yours," she said to the eyes.

She put the light away and headed out of the forest. As she walked among the silent gray forms of the trees, fragments of that other time in the woods came back to her. The cicadas, of course, singing from midday into the evening. The mosquitoes whining at the tender swellings on her head and face. The pain in her stomach. The furry feel of a wet leaf against her tongue. The sticks hurting her bare feet. She remembered things that had seemed like visions: Crows the size of small dogs flapping down into a clearing. A dewy spider web like a shawl of light. Deer in the dusk lifting their narrow, big-eared faces to stare at her, and then leaping silently away, their white tails swallowed by darkness. And she remembered the vision that had seemed real: her mother in her blue waitress uniform kneeling beside her as she lay on the ground. She'd wandered through a dream of revolving night and day, and she would have died in it if a black man and his son hadn't come upon her. The boy looked at her in wide-eyed wonderment, as if she were a ghost, but the man knelt and touched her face. "What happen to you, baby?" he said. "It's awright now. No need to shake." He handed his rifle to the boy and gently picked her up and carried her out of the woods.

But in a sense she'd never left those woods. Not until now, she thought, stepping into the backyard of the house. This was her poem. She got out her cell again, accessed a number, and punched it.

"Cynthia," Jack said in a thick voice.

"Hi. Did I wake you?"

"No, no."

"You can't lie to a cop, you know."

"It's good to hear your voice."

"How are you?"

"Much better, talking to you."

"I wanted you to know you were right about my sleeping problem. It *was* connected to something in the past. And when I admitted that to myself, it got a lot better."

"Good. I'm glad."

"The thing that happened in my past, I'd like to tell you about it sometime."

"Sure. Whenever you want."

"But first I should tell Sally."

"Yes. Where are you—at home?"

"Nope. I'm in the field. Literally. I'm knee-deep in meadow grass."

"What are you doing there?"

"It's a long story, and some other cops are coming. But I can talk until they get here."

"Please."

"You remember those strands of hair?"

"Yes."

She began telling him. It was easy talking to Jack. It was like thinking out loud. She could imagine herself doing it every night.

Acknowledgements

Many thanks to Jeanne Johansen of High Tide Publications for taking a chance on a novice, and to Narielle Living for her editing expertise and tact. Since a book doesn't get written in isolation, except when you're doing the actual writing, there are others I need to thank too: Patricia McCann, for showing me the horse culture of Northern Virginia and reviewing the equine references in the novel; Ralph Ruedy for sharing the details of his fall in the woods; my wife Susan, the kelson of any creation of mine; our daughter Anne, my courage teacher; my sister Susan Witt, who requested a sequel; my mother and father, who would've been pleased; and three supportive and much appreciated readers of the unpublished manuscript: Mary K. Roberts and Victor and Sharon Thompson. Finally, I'd like to express my gratitude to good friends of long acquaintance (you know who you are) who offered encouragement by assuming—seemingly—that I could do it.

About the Author

Scott Butler grew up in Baton Rouge, Louisiana. After graduating from LSU, he earned a doctorate in English at Duke University. He taught literature and film at an eastern Virginia community college for many years. Since his retirement he has devoted his time to writing and to participating in a grassroots effort to preserve Fort Monroe, a former Army post of deep historic significance. He and his wife, Susan, live in Blacksburg, Va.

www.ingramcontent.com/pod-product-compliance
Lightning Source LLC
Chambersburg PA
CBHW061137200626
46817CB00016B/1693